THE
SLOW REGARD
OF SILENT THINGS

PATRICK
ROTHFUSS

ILLUSTRATIONS BY NATE TAYLOR

DAW BOOKS, INC.
DONALD A. WOLLHEIM, FOUNDER
375 Hudson Street, New York, NY 10014
ELIZABETH R. WOLLHEIM
SHEILA E. GILBERT
PUBLISHERS
www.dawbooks.com

First Paperback Printing, November 2015
1 2 3 4 5 6 7 8 9

DAW TRADEMARK REGISTERED
U.S. PAT. AND TM. OFF. AND FOREIGN COUNTRIES
—MARCA REGISTRADA
HECHO EN U.S.A.

PRINTED IN THE U.S.A.

For Vi, without whom there might be no story.
And Tunnel Bob, without whom there would be no Auri.

AUTHOR'S FOREWORD

You might not want to buy this book.

I know, that's not the sort of thing an author is supposed to say. The marketing people aren't going to like this. My editor is going to have a fit. But I'd rather be honest with you right out of the gate.

First, if you haven't read my other books, you don't want to start here.

My first two books are *The Name of the Wind* and *The Wise Man's Fear*. If you're curious to try my writing, start there. They're the best introduction to my world. This book deals with Auri, one of the characters from that series. Without the context of those books, you're probably going to feel pretty lost.

Second, even if you *have* read my other books, I think it's only fair to warn you that this is a bit of a strange story. I don't go in for spoilers, but suffice to say that this one is . . . different. It doesn't do a lot of the things a classic story is supposed to do. And if you're looking for a continuation of Kvothe's storyline, you're not going to find it here.

On the other hand, if you'd like to learn more about Auri, this story has a lot to offer. If you love words and mysteries and secrets. If you're curious about the Underthing and alchemy. If you want to know more about the hidden turnings of my world. . . .

Well, then this book might be for you.

THE FAR BELOW BOTTOM
OF THINGS

WHEN AURI WOKE, she knew that she had seven days.

Yes. She was quite sure of it. He would come for a visit on the seventh day.

A long time. Long for waiting. But not so long for everything that needed to be done. Not if she were careful. Not if she wanted to be ready.

Opening her eyes, Auri saw a whisper of dim light. A rare thing, as she was tucked tidily away in Mantle, her privatest of places. It was a white day, then. A deep day. A finding day. She smiled, excitement fizzing in her chest.

There was just enough light to see the pale shape of her arm as her fingers found the dropper bottle on her bedshelf. She unscrewed it and let a single drip fall into Foxen's dish. After a moment he slowly brightened into a faint gloaming blue.

Moving carefully, Auri pushed back her blanket so it wouldn't touch the floor. She slipped out of bed, the stone floor warm beneath her feet. Her basin rested on the table near her bed, next to a sliver of her sweetest soap. None of it had changed in the night. That was good.

Auri squeezed another drop directly onto Foxen. She hesitated, then grinned and let a third drop fall. No half measures on a finding day. She gathered up her blanket then, folding and folding it up, carefully tucking it under her chin to keep it from brushing against the floor.

Foxen's light continued to swell. First the merest flickering: a fleck, a distant star. Then more of him began to iridesce, a firefly's worth. Still more his brightness grew till he was all-over tremulant with shine. Then he sat proudly in his dish, looking like a blue-green ember slightly larger than a coin.

She smiled at him while he roused himself the rest of the way and he filled all of Mantle with his truest, brightest blue-white light.

Then Auri looked around. She saw her perfect bed. Just her size. Just so. She checked her sitting chair. Her cedar box. Her tiny silver cup.

The fireplace was empty. And above that was the mantelpiece: her yellow leaf, her box of stone, her grey glass jar with sweet dried lavender inside. Nothing was nothing else. Nothing was anything it shouldn't be.

There were three ways out of Mantle. There was a hallway, and a doorway, and a door. The last of these was not for her.

Auri took the doorway into Port. Foxen was still resting in his dish, so his light was dimmer here, but it was still bright enough to see. Port had not been very busy of late, but even so, Auri checked on everything in turn. In the wine rack rested half a broken plate of porcelain, no thicker than the petal of a flower. Below that was a leather octavo book, a pair of corks, a tiny ball of twine. Off to one side, his fine white teacup waited for him with a patience Auri envied.

On the wall shelf sat a blob of yellow resin in a dish. A black rock. A grey stone. A smooth, flat piece of wood. Apart from all the rest, a tiny bottle stood, its wire bale open like a hungry bird.

On the central table a handful of holly berries rested on a clean white cloth. Auri eyed them for a moment, then took them to the bookshelf, a perch they were more suited to. She looked around the room and nodded to herself. All good.

Back in Mantle, Auri washed her face and hands and feet. She slipped out of her nightshirt and folded it into her cedar box. She stretched happily, lifting up her arms and rolling high onto her toes.

Then she ducked into her favorite dress, the one he'd given her. It was sweet against her skin. Her name was burning like a fire inside her. Today was going to be a busy day.

••◦◦◉◦◦••

Auri gathered up Foxen, carrying him cupped in the palm of her hand. She made her way through Port, slipping through a jagged crack in the wall. It was not a wide crack, but Auri was so slight she barely needed turn her shoulders to keep from brushing up against the broken stones. It was nothing like a tight fit.

Van was a tall room with straight, white walls of fitted stone. It was an echo-empty place save for her standing mirror. But today there was one other thing, the gentlest breath of sunlight. It snuck in through the peak of an arched doorway filled with rubble: broken timber, blocks of fallen stone. But there, at the very top, a smudge of light.

Auri stood in front of the mirror and took the bristle brush from where it hung on the mirror's wooden frame. She brushed the sleep snarl from her hair until it hung about her like a cloud.

She closed her hand over Foxen, and without his blue-green shine the room went dark as dark. Then her eyes stretched wide and she could see nothing but the soft, faint smudge of warm light spilling past the rubble high behind her. Pale golden light caught in her pale golden hair. Auri grinned at herself in the mirror. She looked like the sun.

Lifting her hand, she uncovered Foxen and skipped quickly off into the sprawling maze of Rubric. It was barely a minute's work to find a copper pipe with the right kind of cloth wrapping. But finding the perfect *place*, well, that was the trick, wasn't it? She followed the pipe through the round red-brick tunnels for nearly half a mile, careful not to let it slip away from her among the countless other twining pipes.

Then, with no hint of warning, the pipe kinked hard and dove straight into the curving wall, abandoning her. Rude thing. There were countless other pipes of course, but the tiny tin ones had no wrap at all. The icy ones of burnished steel were far too new. The iron pipes were so eager as to be almost embarrassing, but their wrappings were all cotton, and that was more trouble than she cared to bother with today.

So Auri followed a fat ceramic pipe as it bumbled

along. Eventually it burrowed deep into the ground, but where it bent, its linen wrap hung loose and ragged as an urchin's shirt. Auri smiled and unwound the strip of cloth with gentle fingers, taking great care not to tear it.

Eventually it came away. A perfect thing. A single gauzy piece of greying linen, long as Auri's arm. It was tired but willing, and after folding it upon itself she turned and pelted madly off through echoing Umbrel, then down and down into The Twelve.

The Twelve was one of the rare changing places of the Underthing. It was wise enough to know itself, and brave enough to *be* itself, and wild enough to change itself while somehow staying altogether true. It was nearly unique in this regard, and while it was not always safe or kind, Auri could not help but feel a fondness for it.

Today the high arch of space was just as she'd expected, bright and lively. Sunlight speared down through the open gratings far above, striking down into the deep, narrow valley of the changing place. The light filtered past pipes, support beams, and the strong, straight line of an ancient wooden walkway. The distant noise of the street drifted down to the far below bottom of things.

Auri heard the sound of hooves on cobblestones, sharp and round as a cracking knuckle. She heard the distant thunder of a passing wagon and the dim mingle of voices.

Threading through it all was the high, angry cry of a babe who clearly wanted tit and wasn't getting any.

At the bottom of The Yellow Twelve there was a long deep pool with water smooth as glass. The sunlight from above was bright enough that Auri could see all the way down to the second snarl of pipes beneath the surface.

She already had straw here, and three bottles waited on a narrow ledge of stone along one wall. But looking at them, Auri frowned. There was a green one, a brown one, and a clear one. There was a wide wire baling top, a grey twisting lid, and a cork fat as a fist. They were all different shapes and sizes, but none of them were quite right.

Exasperated, Auri threw her hands into the air.

So she ran back to Mantle, her bare feet slapping on the stone. Once there, she eyed the grey glass bottle with the lavender inside. She picked it up, looked it over carefully, then set it back down in its proper place before she scampered out again.

Auri hurried through Port, heading out by way of the slanting doorway this time, rather than the crack in the wall. She twisted up through Withy, Foxen throwing wild shadows on the walls. As she ran, her hair streamed out behind her like a banner.

She took the spiraling stairs through Darkhouse, down and around, down and around. When she finally

heard moving water and the tink of glass she knew she'd crossed the threshold into Clinks. Soon Foxen's light reflected off the roiling pool of black water that swallowed the bottom of the spiraling stairs.

There were two bottles perched in a shallow niche there. One blue and narrow. One green and squat. Auri tilted her head and closed one eye, then reached out to touch the green one with two fingers. She grinned, snatched it up, and ran back up the stairs.

Heading back, she went through Vaults for a change of air. Running down the hall, she sprang over the first deep fissure in the broken floor as lithely as a dancer. The second crack she leapt as lightly as a bird. The third she jumped as wildly as a pretty girl who looked like the sun.

She came into The Yellow Twelve all puffed and panting. As she caught her breath, she tucked Foxen in the green bottle, padded him carefully with straw, and locked down the hasp against the rubber gasket, sealing the lid down tight. She held it up to her face, then grinned and kissed the bottle before setting it carefully by the edge of the pool.

Auri shucked off her favorite dress and hung it on a bright brass pipe. She grinned and shivered a little, nervous fish swimming in her stomach. Then, standing in her altogether, she gathered up her floating hair with both her hands. She brushed it back and bound it, winding and tying it behind her with the strip of old grey linen cloth. When she was done it made a long tail that hung down to the small of her back.

Arms held close against her chest, Auri took two tiny steps to stand beside the pool. She dipped a toe into the water, then her whole foot. She grinned at the feel of it, chill and sweet as peppermint. Then she lowered herself down, both legs dangling in the water. Auri balanced for a moment, holding her nekkid self up with both hands, away from the cold stone lip at the edge of the pool.

But there was no avoiding it. So Auri puckered up and settled herself the rest of the way down. There was nothing peppermint about the cold stone edge. It was a dull, blunt bite against her tender altogether hindmost self.

She turned herself around then, and began to lower herself into the water. She went slowly, tickling around with her feet until she found the little jut of stone. She curled her toes around it, holding herself thigh-deep in the pool. Then she drew a few deep breaths, screwed her eyes shut, and bared her teeth before letting go with her toes and ducking her nethers underneath the surface. She squeaked a little, and the chill made her whole self go gooseprickle.

The worst over, she closed her eyes and dunked her head beneath the water too. Gasping and blinking, she rubbed the water out of her eyes. She had her big all-over shiver then, one arm folded across her breasts.

But by the time it was done her grimace had turned to grin.

Without her halo of hair, Auri felt small. Not the smallness that she strove for every day. Not the smallness of a tree among trees. Of a shadow underground. And not just small of body either. She knew there was not much of her. When she thought to look more closely at her standing mirror, the girl she saw was tiny as an urchin begging on the street. The girl she saw was thin as thin. Her cheekbones high and delicate. Her collarbones pressed tight against her skin.

But no. With her hair pulled back and wetted down besides. She felt . . . less. She felt tamped down. Dim. More faint. Feint. Feigned. Fain. It would have been pure unpleasant without the perfect strip of linen. If not for that, she wouldn't merely feel like a wick rolled down, she would be downright guttery. It was worth it, doing things the proper way.

Finally the last of her trembling stopped. The fish were still turning in her stomach, but her grin was eager. The golden daylight from above struck down into the pool, straight and bright and steady as a spear.

Auri drew a deep breath, then pushed it out, wriggling her toes. She took another deep breath and let it out more slowly.

Then a third breath. Auri gripped the neck of Foxen's bottle in one hand, let go of the stone edge of the pool, and dove beneath the water.

••••••••••

The angle of the light was perfect, and Auri saw the first pipetangle clear as anything. Minnow-quick, she turned and glided smoothly through, not letting any of them touch her.

Below that was the second snarl. She pushed an old iron pipe with her foot to keep herself moving downward, then tugged a valve with her free hand as she went past, changing speed and sliding through the narrow space between two wrist-thick copper pipes.

The spearlight faded as she sank, leaving only Foxen's blue-green glow. But his light was muted here, filtered through straw and water and the thick green glass. Auri made her mouth a perfect O and puffed out two quick bursts of bubbles. The pressure grew as she went deeper, shapes looming dimly by her in the dark. An old walkway, a tilting slab of rock, an ancient, algae-covered wooden beam.

Her outstretched fingers found the bottom sooner than her eyes, and Auri swept her hand across the half-seen surface of the smooth stone floor. Back and forth. Back and forth. Quick but wary. Sometimes there were sharp things here.

Then her fingers closed on something long and smooth. A stick? She tucked it underneath her arm and let herself begin to float back up toward the distant light. Her free hand found familiar pipes, pulling and steering, twisting through the maze of half-seen shapes. Her lungs began to ache a bit, and she released a stream of bubbles as she rose.

Her face broke the surface near the edge, and in the golden light she saw what she had found: a clean white bone. Long, but not a leg. An arm. The prima axial. She ran her fingers down the length of it and felt a tiny seam that ran all round it like a ring, showing it had broken and long-healed. It was full of pleasant shadows.

Smiling, Auri set it aside. Then she drew three slow, deep breaths, gripped Foxen tight, and dove into the pool again.

This time she got her foot wedged tight between two pipes around the second tangle. Bad luck. She scowled and tugged and after half a moment managed to pull free. She blew half her lungful out and kicked hard, dropping like a stone down into the black below.

Despite the bad start, this was an easy catch. Her fingers found a tangle of something-or-other before they even touched the bottom. She had no guess what it might be. Something metal, something slick and something hard all jumbled up together. She gathered it close to her chest and started up again.

This time she couldn't tuck her find beneath her arm for fear she'd lose some piece of it. So Auri nestled Foxen's bottle in the crook of her arm and pulled herself along with her left hand. It felt good, balanced, and she broke the surface not even needing to blow the rest of her bubbles.

She spread the tangle out by the edge of the pool: an old belt with a silver buckle so tarnished it was black as coal. A leafy branch with a bewildered snail. And, lastly but not least, looped on a piece of rotten string all tangled with the branch, was a slender key as long as her first finger.

Auri kissed the snail and apologized before setting the branch back in the water where it belonged. The leather of the belt was turned against itself, but at the slightest tug the buckle came away. Both of them were better off that way.

Clinging to the stone edge of the pool, Auri shivered now in tiny waves. They moved across her shoulders and her chest. Her lips had gone from pink to pale pink tinged with blue.

She picked up Foxen's bottle and checked the bale to make sure it was tight. She looked down into the water, the fish in her stomach swimming excitedly. Third time was the lucky one.

Auri pulled a breath and dove again, her body twisting smoothly, her right hand finding all the friendly grips. Down to the dark. The stone. The timber. Then nothing but dim Foxen's light, coloring her outstretched hand a pale blue-green. It looked the way a water nixie's must.

Her knuckles brushed the bottom and she spun a bit to orient herself. She kicked and swept her hand about, skimming smoothly out along the black stone bottom of the pool. Then she saw a glint of light and her fingers bumped something solid and cold, all hard lines and smooth. It was full of love and answers, so full she felt them spilling out at just her briefest touch.

For the space of ten hard heartbeats Auri thought it must be fastened to the stone. Then it slid and she realized the truth. It was a weighty thing. After a long, slippery moment her tiny fingers found a way to pry it up. It was solid metal, thick as a book. It was oddly shaped and heavy as a bar of raw iridium.

Auri brought it to her chest and felt its edges dig into her skin. Then she bent her knees and pushed off hard against the bottom with both feet, looking up toward the distant shimmer of the surface.

She kicked and kicked, but barely seemed to move. The metal thing dragged, pulling her down. Her foot bumped hard against a thick iron pipe, and Auri took the chance to brace herself and give another push. She felt a rush of motion up that slowed as soon as her foot left the iron behind.

Her lungs were fighting with her now. Half-full, the dumb things wanted air. She puffed out a mouthful of bubbles, trying to trick them, knowing every bubble lost would weigh her down, knowing she wasn't even near the bottom tangle yet.

Auri tried to shift the metal thing to the crook of her arm so she could pull herself along. But when she tried, the smoothness of it slipped a little in her fingers. In the sudden panic afterward, she clutched, fumbled, and Foxen's bottle knocked against some unseen shape. He slid and jostled free of Auri's grip.

Auri snatched with her free hand, but her knuckles only batted Foxen farther off away. And for a moment, Auri froze. To let the metal drop would be unthinkable. But Foxen. He had been with her forever. . . .

She watched as Foxen's bottle was caught by an eddy and swirled well out of reach behind a trio of slanting copper pipes. Her lungs were angry now. She clenched her teeth and grabbed a nearby lip of stone with her now-free hand, pulling herself up.

Her lungs were heaving hard inside her now, so she slowly loosed her bubbles though she hadn't even glimpsed the lowest tangle yet. It was dark without Foxen, but at least she was moving, pulling herself up in sudden awkward jerks, using whatever strange handholds she could find. She kicked, but there was little to be gained from that, burdened as she was with the heavy lump of sharp, hard love she held so tightly to her chest. Was it the answers that it held that gave it so much weight?

Finally she dragged herself into the lower nest of pipes, but her lungs were empty now, and her body hung like lead. Normally she twisted through the tangle like a fish, her body never brushing the pipes. But she was heavy and empty. One-handed she groped and bucked her way through them. She banged her knee and frantically slid her back along something sharp

with rust. She stretched out an arm, but heavy as she was, her fingers didn't even brush her usual handhold.

She kicked, gained another inch or two, then, despite her careful binding, her hair snagged on something. It jerked her to a sudden stop, snapping her head back and spinning her body sideways in the water.

Almost immediately she felt herself begin to sink. She flailed out wildly. Her shin struck a pipe, making her whole self tingle with pain, but she quickly sought it out with her other foot, braced, and shoved off *hard*. She shot up like a cork, fast enough so that her hair tore free from whatever rude thing had caught it. The sharp tug snapped her head back hard, forcing her mouth open.

She began to drown then. Mouth full of water, she choked and gagged. But even as the water filled her nose and throat, Auri feared nothing so much as the thought her hand might slip, that she would lose her grip and let the heavy jag of metal slide away into the dark. Losing Foxen was bad. It would leave her blind and lonely in the dark. Being trapped beneath the pipes and choking out her life was awful too. But neither of those things were *wrong*. Letting the metal slide into the dark simply could not be done. It was unthinkable. It was so unkilter that it terrified her.

Her hair was unbound now, and it swirled around her in the water like a cloud of smoke. Her hand grabbed a curve of pipe, comforting, familiar. She pulled herself up, then grabbed again and found another grip. She clenched her teeth, choked, pulled, and grabbed.

She broke the surface, gasping and spluttering, then slid under the water again.

A second later she claw-clambered her way up again. This time her free hand caught the stone edge of the pool.

Auri heaved the thing out of the water, and it struck the stone floor with the sound of a bell. It was a bright brass gear, big as a platter. Thicker than her thumb with some to spare. It had a hole in the middle, nine teeth, and a jagged gap where a tenth had long ago been torn away.

It was full of true answers and love and hearthlight. It was beautiful.

Auri smiled and heaved up half a stomachful of water on the stones. Then heaved again, turning her head so that it didn't splash against the bright brass

gear. She coughed then, took a mouthful of water, and spat it back into the pool. The brass gear lay heavy as a heart on the cold stones of The Yellow Twelve. The light from up above made the surface of it shimmerant and gold. It looked like a piece of sun she'd brought up from the deep.

Auri coughed again and shivered. Then she reached out and touched it with one finger. She smiled to look at it. Her lips were blue. She trembled. Her heart was full of joy.

●●●◗◍◖●●●

After she pulled herself out of the water, Auri looked around the pool at the bottom of The Twelve. Though she knew better, she hoped to see Foxen bobbing idly on the surface.

Nothing.

Her face was solemn then. She thought of going back. But no. Three times. That was the way of things. But the thought of leaving Foxen in the dark was enough to put a fine, thin crack straight through her heart. To lose him after all this time. . . .

Then Auri caught a glimpse of something deep below the surface. A glint. A glow. She grinned. Foxen looked for all the world like a great bumbrous firefly as he bobbled and bumped his slow way slowly up through all the tangled pipes.

She waited five long minutes, watching Foxen's

bottle bob and drift until it finally popped up to the surface like a duck. Then she caught it up and kissed it. She held it to her chest. Oh yes. It was well worth it, doing things the proper way.

•••◦◉◦•••

First things first. Auri freed Foxen from the bottle and set it next to the others on the wall. Then she headed down to Clinks and rinsed herself in the roiling water there. Then she washed herself, using up the slender remnant of a cake of soap that smelled of cinnas fruit and summer.

After soaping and scrubbing and cleaning her hair, Auri dove into the endless black water of Clinks to rinse herself one final time. Under the surface, something brushed against her. Something slick and heavy pressed its moving weight against her leg. It did not bother her. Whatever it was, it was in its proper place and so was she. Things were just as they should be.

Dripping clean and wringing out her hair, Auri headed off through Tenners. Not the quickest way, but it would be unseemly to head through Dunnings in nothing but her pinkness. But even taking the longer way, it wasn't long before she turned the corner into Bakers, wet feet slapping on the stone. She rested Foxen on a piece of jutting brick nearby, as he wasn't fond of too much heat.

The thick steel pipes along the tunnel's wall were too hot to stand near today, and the walls and floor had been basking until they too were all crickly with heat.

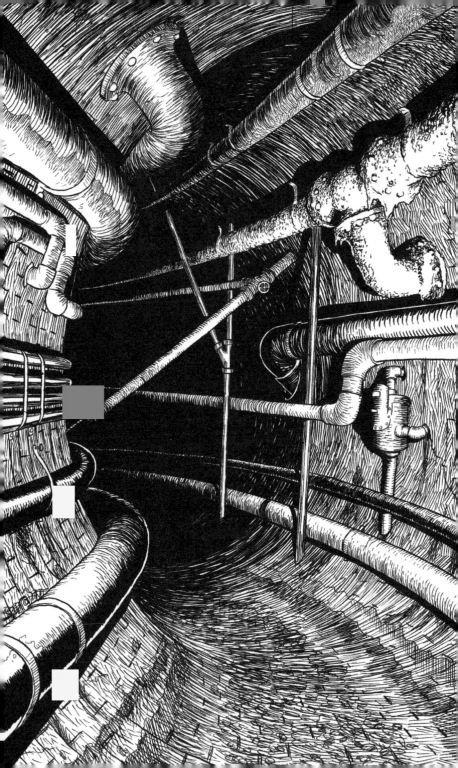

Auri spun in a slow circle to keep any part of her tender altogether from getting roasted by the silent red roar pouring off the pipes. It was only moments before the place had dried her skin, set her fine hair floating, and cooked the shivers from her icy bones.

After that she fetched her favorite dress from The Yellow Twelve. She slid it over her head, then carried all her treasures back to Port where she arranged them on the central table.

The leather belt was etched in odd curling patterns. The great brass gear was bright straight through. The key was black as black. The buckle though, it was black with bright beneath. It was a hidden thing.

Might the buckle be for him? That would be a good beginning to the day. A nice thing to have settled early on, his gift all ready with his visit days away.

Auri eyed the buckle sharply. Was it a proper gift for him? He *was* a tangled sort. And he was much hidden, too. Nodding, she reached out to touch the cool dark metal.

But no. It didn't suit him. She should have known. He was not a one for fastening. For holding closed. Neither was he dark. Oh no. He was emberant. Incarnadine. He was bright with better bright beneath, like copper-gilded gold.

The gear would need consideration. It almost felt like it could be for him—but that could wait. The key needed urgent tending. It was for certain the most restless of the lot. This wasn't even a slim sliver of surprise. Keys were hardly known for their complacency, and this one was near howling for a lock. Auri picked it up and turned it in her hands. A door key. It wasn't shy about the fact at all.

Black key. White day. She cocked her head. The shape of things was right. It was a finding day, and there was no doubt the poor thing badly wanted tending. She nodded to herself and slipped the key into the pocket of her dress.

Even so, before she left, Auri helped everything to find its proper place. The belt stayed on the central table, obviously. The buckle moved to rest beside the dish of resin. The bone nestled almost indecently close to the holly berry.

The gear was troublesome in this regard. She set it on the bookshelf, then moved it to the table in the corner. It leaned against the wall, the gap from its lost tooth pointing up into the air. Auri frowned. It wasn't quite the proper place.

Auri brought out the key and held it in front of the gear. Black and brass. Both for turning. They had twelve teeth between them. . . .

She shook her head and sighed. She put the key back into her pocket and left the great brass gear on the bookshelf. It wasn't the proper place for it, but it was the best that she could do for now.

•••◗◗•••

Borough was closest, so Auri hurried there, ducking her head through the low stone doorways until she came to the first of its doors. Standing there, Auri cupped Foxen in her palm and huffed a gentle breath onto him, fanning his light. The wooden door was huge and grey with age, its hinges hardly more than flaking rust.

She drew the key out of her pocket and held it out in front of her, between herself and the great grey door. She looked back and forth between them, then turned and padded away. Three left turns and through a broken window to the second door, also old and grey, but larger than the first. Here she barely needed to glance at them before she knew the truth. This wasn't right. These weren't the proper doors. Where then? Tenners? Black Door?

She shivered. Not Black Door. Not on a white day. Wains instead. Then Tenners. Even Throughbottom. This was not a key for Black Door. No.

Auri hurried through Rubric, turning left twice and right twice for balance, making sure to never follow any of the pipes too far lest she offend. Next came Greely with its twisting ways and its sulfurant smell. She got a little lost there among the crumbling walls, but eventually made her right way to Crumbledon, a narrow dirt tunnel so steep it was little more than a hole. Auri scampered down on a long ladder made of lashed-together sticks.

The bottom of the ladder dropped into a tiny, tidy room of finished stone. It was no bigger than a closet, empty except for an old oak door all bound in brass. Auri brushed off her hands, swung the door open, and stepped lightly into Wains.

The hallway was wide enough to drive a wagon through. High-ceilinged and long enough that Foxen's light could barely reach the tangle of debris that blocked the far end. Above her, blue-white light scattered off a crystal chandelier.

Dark wood paneling hugged the lower portion of the walls, but above that was ornate plasterwork. There were broad frescoes decorating the ceiling. Women in gauze lounged about, whispering and rubbing oil on each other. Men frolicked about in the water, flapping around ridiculously in their absolute altogether.

Auri took a moment to look at the pictures as she always did, grinning wickedly. She shifted her weight from side to side, the polished marble floor chill beneath her tiny feet.

Both ends of Wains were blocked by fallen rock and earth, but in the middle it was clean as a crucible. Everything dry and tight as you please. No damp. No mold. No drafts to bring in dust. Altogether men or no, it was a seemly place, so Auri was careful to comport herself with full decorum.

There were twelve oak doors lining the hall. All fine and tight and bound in brass. Over her long years in the Underthing, Auri had opened three of them.

She walked down the hall, Foxen glowing brightly

in her upheld hand. After a dozen steps, a glimmer on the marble floor caught her eye. Skipping close, she saw a crystal had fallen from the chandelier to lay unbroken on the floor. It was a lucky thing, and brave. She picked it up and put it in the pocket that didn't have the key inside. They would only fuss if they were put together.

It wasn't the third door, or the seventh. Auri was already planning her route down to Throughbottom when she spied the ninth door. It was waiting. Eager. The latch turned and the door eased smoothly open on silent hinges.

Auri stepped inside, pulled the key from her pocket, and kissed it before she lay it carefully on an empty table just inside the door. The tiny tap as it touched the wood warmed her heart. She smiled to see it sitting there, all snug and in its proper place.

It was a sitting room. Very fine. Auri sat Foxen in a wall sconce and went to have a careful look around. A tall velvet chair. A low wooden table. A plush couch on a plush carpet. In the corner was a tiny cart filled with glasses and bottles. They were very dignified.

There was something wrong with the room. Nothing looming. Nothing like in Sit Twice or Faceling. No. This was a good place. A nearly perfect place. Everything was almost. If this hadn't been a white day with

27

everything done properly, she might not have been able to tell something was amiss. Still, it was, and she did.

Auri stepped around the room, hands clasped primly behind her back. She eyed the cart, more than a dozen bottles, all colors. Some stoppered and full, some holding little more than dust. There was a burnished silver gear watch on one of the tables, near the couch. There was a ring too, and a scattering of coins. Auri eyed them curiously, touching nothing.

She moved daintily. One step. Another. The dark plush of the carpet was sweet beneath her feet, like moss, and when she bent down to run her fingers over the hush of it, she glimpsed a tiny whiteness underneath the couch. She reached deep into the shadows with a small white hand, having to stretch a bit before her fingers caught it. Smooth and cool.

It was a tiny figurine carved from a piece of pale, retiring stone. A small soldier with clever lines to show his hauberk and his shield. But his truest treasure was the sweetness of his face, kind enough for kissing.

It didn't belong here, but it wasn't wrong. Or rather, it wasn't what was wrong with the room. The poor thing was simply lost. Auri smiled and put the doll in her pocket with the crystal.

It was then she felt a tiny bump beneath one foot. She pulled up the edge of the carpet, rolled it back, and found a small bone button underneath. Auri eyed it for a long moment before giving it an understanding smile.

That wasn't it either. The button was just as it should be. Moving carefully, she lay the carpet back exactly as she'd found it, patting it into place with her hands.

She looked around the room again. It was a good place, and almost entirely as it ought to be. There wasn't really anything for her to do here. It was startling really, as the place had obviously been alone for ages without anyone tending to it.

Even so, there *was* something wrong. Some lack. Some tiny thing, like a single cricket legging madly in the night.

A second door sat on the other side of the room, eager to be opened. She worked the latch, walked through a hallway, only to come to the foot of a set of stairs. There she looked around with some surprise. She'd thought that she was still in Wains. But clearly not. This was a different place entirely.

Auri's heart beat faster then. It had been ages since she'd come on somewhere wholly new. A place that dared to be entirely itself.

Still, carefully. In Foxen's steady light Auri looked closely at the walls and ceiling. A few cracks, but nothing thicker than a thumb. A few small stones had fallen, and there was dirt and mortar on the steps as well. The walls were bare and slightly condescending. No. She had obviously left Wains behind.

She ran a hand over the stones of the steps. The first few were solid, but the fourth was loose. As were the sixth and seventh. And the tenth.

There was a landing halfway up where the stairway turned back upon itself. There was a door, but it was terribly bashful, so Auri politely pretended not to see it. She made her careful way up the second flight of steps and found half of them were also loose or prone to tipping.

Then she went back down the stairs, making sure she'd found all the shifting stones. She hadn't. It was terribly exciting. The place was tricky as a drunken tinker and a little sly. It had a temper too. It would be hard to find a place less like a garden path.

Some places had names. Some places changed, or they were shy about their names. Some places had no names at all, and that was always sad. It was one thing to be private. But to have no name at all? How horrible. How lonely.

Auri made her way up the stairs a second time, testing each one with her feet, avoiding the spots she knew were bad. As she climbed, she couldn't tell what sort of place this was. Shy or secret? Lost or lonely? A puzzling place. It made her grin all the wider.

⋯⋅❁⋅⋯

At the top of the stairs the ceiling had collapsed, but there was a gap made by a broken wall. Auri stepped through and found herself grinning with the thrill of it. Another new place. Two in one day. Her bare feet shifted back and forth on the gritty stone floor, almost dancing with excitement.

This place was not so coy as the stairway. Its name was Tumbrel. It was scattered and half-fallen and half-full. There was so much to see.

Half the ceiling had fallen in and everything was covered in dust. But for all its fallen stone, it was dry and tight. No damp, just dust and stiff air. More than half the room was a solid mass of fallen earth and stone and timber. The remnants of a four-post bed lay crushed beneath the wreckage. In the unfallen portion of the room, there was a triune mirror vanity and a dark wooden wardrobe taller than a tall woman standing on her toes.

Auri peered shyly through the wardrobe's half-open doors. She glimpsed a dozen dresses there, all velvet and embroidery. Shoes. A robe of silk. Some gauzy bits of the sort the women wore in the frescoes down in Wains.

The vanity was a rakish thing: garrulous and un-ashamed. The top was scattered with pots of powders, small brushes, sticks of eyepaint. Bracelets and rings. Combs of horn and ivory and wood. There were pins and pens and a dozen bottles, some substantial, some delicate as petals.

It was in startling disarray. Everything resting atop the vanity was somehow askew: powders were spilled, bottles toppled, the dish of pins all higgledy-piggledy.

Dishevel or no, Auri couldn't help but take a liking to the thing, gruff and bawdy as it was. She sat primly on the edge of the straight-backed chair. She ran her fingers through her floating hair and smiled to see her self reflected in a triptych.

There was a door too, opposite the broken wall. It was half-buried by a broken beam and blocks of shattered stone. But hidden as it was, it wasn't shy.

Auri went to work then, setting things to rights as best she could.

She shifted the wooden beam that blocked the door. Lifting and straining, a few inches at a time until she could lever at it with another piece of fallen timber. Then she cleared away the stones, pushing the ones she could not carry. Rolling the ones she could not push.

She found the wreckage of a small table underneath the stones, and amid the splintered wood she found a length of fine white tatted lace. She folded this up carefully and put it in her pocket with the crystal and the small stone soldier.

Once the way was clear, the door pulled open easily, its rusted hinges moaning. Inside was a small closet. There was an empty porcelain chamberpot. There was a wooden bucket, a brush of the sort you would use to scrub the deck of a ship, and a tight birch broom. On the back of the door hung two empty linen sacks. The smaller of these was anxious to be about its business, so Auri smiled and tucked it in a pocket by itself.

The broom was eager after being trapped so long, so Auri brought it out and set to sweeping, brushing ancient dust and earth into a tidy pile. After that it was still restless, so Auri went to sweep the unnamed stair as well.

She brought Foxen with, of course. She would hardly trust a place like that to behave in the dark. But since a proper birching of the place required two hands, Auri tied Foxen to a long lock of her hanging hair. Foxen's dignity was somewhat bruised by this, and Auri kissed him in sincere apology for the affront. But they both knew he took a certain secret joy from swingling wildly all about, making the shadows spin and skirl.

So for a while he hung and swung. Auri took care not to notice any undue exuberance on his part while she gave the unnamed stairs a brisk once-over. Up and down then up again, the tight birch broom flicked and tickled the stone steps clear of fallen rocks and grit and dust. They were flattered by the attention while remaining entirely coy.

After returning the broom to the closet, Auri brought out the chamberpot and set it near the wardrobe. She spun it slightly so it faced the proper way.

Charming as it was, the vanity was vexing, too. It seemed all askew, but nothing called out for tidying. The only exception was the hairbrush, which she moved closer to a cunning ruby ring.

Auri crossed her arms and stared at the vanity for a long minute. Then she went down on hands and knees and looked at its underside. She opened the drawers and moved the handkerchiefs from the left-hand drawer into the right, then frowned and moved them back again.

Finally she pushed the entire thing about two hand-span to the left and slightly closer to the wall, careful not to let anything tumble to the floor. She slid the vanity's high-backed chair the same amount, so it still faced the mirrors. Then she picked up the chair and examined the bottoms of its feet before putting it back in place with a tiny shrug.

There was a loose stone in the floor next to the wardrobe. Auri prized it up with her fingers, adjusted the small leather sack and piece of wool padding underneath, then slid the stone back into place, tamping it down firmly with the handle of the broom. She tested it with one foot and smiled when it no longer shifted under her weight.

Lastly, she opened the wardrobe. She moved the dress of burgundy velvet away from the gown of pale blue silk. She replaced the lid of a tall hatbox that had come ajar. She opened the drawer at the bottom of the wardrobe.

Her breath caught in her chest then. Folded tidily away at the bottom of the drawer were several perfect sheets, pale and smooth. Auri reached down to touch one and was amazed at the tightness of the weave. So fine her fingers couldn't feel the thread. It was cool and sweet to the touch, like a lover come to kiss her, fresh in from the cold.

Auri brushed her hand across the surface. How lovely might it be to sleep on such a sheet? To lay on it and feel the sweetness of it all along her naked skin?

She shivered, and her fingers curled around the folded edges of the sheet. Hardly realizing what she did, she drew it from its proper place and brought it to her chest. She brushed her lips against its smoothness. There were other sheets beneath it. A treasure trove. Surely enough for a place like Tumbrel. Besides, she'd set so many other things to rights. Surely . . .

She looked down at the sheet for a long moment. And while her eyes were all softness and want, her mouth grew firm and furious. No. That was not the way of things. She knew better. She knew perfectly well where this sheet belonged.

Auri closed her eyes and put the sheet back in the drawer, shame burning in her chest. She was a greedy thing sometimes. Wanting for herself. Twisting the world all out of proper shape. Pushing everything about with the weight of her desire.

She closed the drawer and came to her feet. Looking around, she nodded to herself. She'd made a good beginning here. The vanity was obviously in need of some attention, but she couldn't taste the nature of it yet. Still, the place had a name and everything obvious was tended to.

Auri took Foxen and headed down the unnamed stair, through Wains and Crumbledon and all the way back to Mantle. She fetched fresh water. She washed her face and hands and feet.

After that she felt much better. She grinned, and on a whim she sprinted off to Delving. She hadn't visited in ages and missed the warm earth smell of it. The closeness of the walls.

Running lightly on her toes, Auri danced through Rubric, ducking pipes. She skipped through Woods, reaching out to swing herself from time-worn beams that held the sagging roof at bay. Finally she came to a swollen wooden door.

Stepping through, she held Foxen high. She smelled the air. She grinned. She knew exactly where she was. Everything was just where it should be.

WHAT A LOOK ENTAILS

THE SECOND DAY, Auri woke to silence in the perfect dark.

That meant a turning day. A doing day. Good. There was much to do before he came. She wasn't nearly ready.

She roused Foxen and folded up her blanket, careful to keep the corners off the floor. She glanced around the room, her box and leaf and lavender were fine. Her bed was fine. Everything was just as it should be.

There were three ways out of Mantle. The hallway was for later. The doorway was for now. The door was oak, bound in iron. Auri did not look at it.

In Port the stone figurine and the length of lace had made themselves at home. The brave crystal was content in the wine rack. The arm bone and linen sack were so comfortable you'd think they'd been there for a hundred years. The old black buckle was crowding the resin a bit, but that was quickly mended. She nudged it to one side to keep things civilized.

She looked around and sighed. Everything was fine except for the great brass gear. It exasperated her.

She picked the crystal up and set it next to the gear. But that didn't help at all and just upset the crystal. It was brave enough for ten, but it wasn't for the corner table. She gave it a quick kiss by way of apology and returned it to the wine rack.

Auri picked up the heavy gear with both hands and brought it into Mantle. It was unheard of, really, but by this point she was at something of a loss. She set it on the narrow ledge of stone on the wall opposite her bed. She tipped it so the empty gap its missing tooth made was straight up toward the ceiling. As if it were reaching upward with its too-short stubby arms.

Stepping back, she looked at it and sighed. Better. But even so, it wasn't quite the proper place.

Auri washed her face and hands and feet. Her thin sliver of soap smelled of sunlight and that made her smile. Then she slipped into her second favorite dress, as it had better pockets. It was a turning day, after all.

In Port she put her linen gathersack over one shoulder, tucking a few things inside. Then she packed her pockets full as full. Before she left, Auri glanced back into Mantle at the brazen gear. But no. If it had wanted to come, it should have been content to stay in Port. Proud thing.

In Van she was startled to find the mirror was unsettled. Anxious even. Hardly an auspicious start to her day. Still, it was the sort of thing only a fool would willfully ignore. And Auri was no fool.

Besides, the mirror had been around for quite a while, so she knew its little ways. It wanted moving, but it needed to be settled first. It needed to be comforted. Coaxed. It needed covering. So, despite the fact that she was yet unbrushed, Auri gathered up Foxen and took the long way down to Wains, walking slowly to her newly opened door as she eyed the frescoes overhead.

She stopped briefly in the sitting room, looking around. The tiny wrongness was still there, like a hint of gristle in her teeth. It wouldn't bother her if everything else here wasn't almost circle perfect.

But some things simply can't be rushed. Auri knew this for a fact. Besides, she needed the mirror set to rights before anything else. That meant covering. So she headed up the unnamed stair, her feet skipping back and forth to miss the unsafe stones. Then she headed through the broken wall and into Tumbrel.

Once there, Auri opened up the wardrobe's drawer. She did not touch the sheets, instead her hands went to her pockets. She felt the smooth facets of the brave crystal. No. She touched the curved lines of the kind stone figurine. No. The flat black rock? No.

Then her fingers touched the buckle and she smiled. She brought it out and set it gently in the drawer. Then she lifted out the topmost folded sheet. It was smooth and creamy in her hands. Pale as ivory.

Auri stopped then, looking at the blackness of the buckle in the drawer. There was a stone in her stomach. It didn't belong here. Oh it *seemed* sensible. Oh yes. Certainly. But she knew what seeming was worth in the end, didn't she?

Reluctantly, she lay the sheet back in the drawer, her fingers ran over its perfect whiteness, smooth and clean and new. There was a hint of winter in it.

But no. There is a difference between the truth and what we wish were true. Sighing, Auri took the buckle back and pushed it deep into her pocket.

Leaving the sheet where it was, Auri headed back to Mantle. She moved more slowly now, no skipping. The trip down the unnamed stair cheered her somewhat. Her path staggered drunkenly back and forth as she moved from one safe section to another.

A stone turned underneath her feet, and Auri pin-wheeled her arms to keep from slipping. She cocked her head to the side, standing balanced on one foot. Was this place Tipple then? No. It was too sly for that.

The mirror was still restless back in Van. And with no better options, Auri was forced to fetch her blanket from her bed. Careful not to let it touch the ground, she draped it over the mirror before turning it to face the wall. Only then could it be moved across the room so that it stood before the bricked-over window where it so desperately wanted to be.

She returned her blanket to Mantle and washed her face and hands and feet. Coming back to Van, she saw her time had been well spent. She'd never seen her mirror so content. Grinning at herself, she brushed the elf knots from her hair until it hung around her like a golden cloud.

But just as she was finishing, when she lifted up her arms to push her cloud of hair behind her, Auri staggered just a bit, all sudden dizzy. After it passed, she walked slowly to Cricklet and took a long, deep drink. She felt the cool water run all along her insides with nothing to stop it. She felt hollow inside. Her stomach was an empty fist.

Her feet wanted to go to Applecourt, but she knew there were no apples left. He wouldn't be waiting there, anyway. Not until the seventh day. Which was good, really. She had nothing suitable to share. Nor nothing halfway good enough to be a proper gift.

So she went to Tree instead. Her pans were hanging in their proper places. Her spirit lamp just so. The cracked clay cup was sitting quietly. Everything was just as it should be.

That said, she had more tools than food in Tree. On the shelves there was the sack of salt he'd given her. There were four fat figs swaddled modestly in a sheet of folded paper. A single, lonely, withered apple. A hand-

ful of dried peas sat sadly at
the bottom of a clear glass jar.

Set into the stone counter was a chill-
well, running with a slow but constant stream of
icy water. But it was keeping nothing cool save for a
lump of yellow butter, and that was full of knives,
scarcely fit for eating.

On the counter was a fine and wondrous thing. A
silver bowl, all brimming full of nutmeg pittems. Round
and brown and smooth as river stones, they had come
visiting from long-off lands. They filled the air, almost
singing of their faraway. Auri eyed them longingly and
ran her fingertips along the edge of their silver bowl. It
was etched with twining leaves. . . .

But no. Rare and lovely as they were, she did not
think they would be good for eating. Not now at any

rate. In that way they were like the butter, not food exactly. They were mysteries that wished to bide their time in Tree.

Auri climbed onto the stone counter so she could reach the apple where it perched up high upon its shelf. Then she sat next to the chill-well, cross-legged, back straight, and cut the apple into seven equal pieces before eating it. It was leathery and full of autumn.

After that she was still hungry, so she brought down the paper and lay it in front of herself, unfolding it carefully. Then she ate three of the figs, taking dainty bites and humming to herself. By the time she finished, her hands weren't shaking any more. She wrapped the single fig back up and set it on the shelf, then climbed down to the floor. She cupped some water from the well and drank it. She grinned. It gave her belly shivers.

••◦◖◗◦••

After eating, Auri knew it was past time she found the brazen gear its proper place.

She tried to flatter it at first. Using both hands, she sat it carefully atop the mantelpiece beside her box of stone. It ignored the compliment and simply sat there, not one bit more forthcoming than it had been before.

Sighing, Auri picked it up with both hands and carried it to Umbrel, but it wasn't happy in amongst the ancient barrels there. Neither did it want to rest in

43

Cricklet near the stream. She carried it through all of Darkhouse, setting it on every windowsill, but none of them suited it in the least.

Arms growing sore from the weight of it, Auri tried to be irritated, but she couldn't stay angry. The gear was unlike anything she had ever seen before in all her years below. Just looking at it made her happy. And heavy as it was, it was a joy to touch. It was a sweet thing. A silent bell that struck out love. All the while she carried it, it sang through her fingers of the secret answers that it held.

No. She couldn't be angry. It was doing everything it could. It was her own fault for not knowing where it belonged. Answers were always important, but they were seldom easy. She would simply have to take her time and do things in the proper way.

Just to be sure, Auri carried the gear back to where she'd found it. She would be sad to see it go, but sometimes there was nothing else to do. Some things simply were too true to stay. Some merely came to visit for a while.

As Auri stepped inside the arching darkness of The Grey Twelve, Foxen's light stretched up toward the unseen ceiling. His calm green glow reached out between the pipes that tangled on the walls. This was a different place today. That was its nature. Even so, Auri knew that she was welcome here. Or, if not welcome, at least indifferently ignored.

Auri made her way farther into the room, where the

deep black water of the pool lay smooth as glass. Carefully, she set the bright gear upright on the stone edge of pool, the gap from its broken tooth faced upward at an angle. She took a step back and covered Foxen with one hand. With nothing but the dim grey light from the grate above, the gear was nowhere near as shimmerant as it had been before. She eyed it closely for a breathless moment, head tilted to one side.

Then she grinned. It didn't want to leave. That at least was clear. She picked it up and tried it on the narrow ledge above the pool beside her bottles. But it simply sat there, all aloof, coruscant with answers, taunting her.

Auri sat cross-legged on the floor and tried to think what other place might fit the brazen gear. Mandril? Candlebear? She heard a hush of feather in the air. Wings beat hard, then stopped. Looking up, Auri saw the shape of a nightjar outlined against the dull grey circle of light entering the grate high above.

The bird struck something hard against the pipe, then ate it. A snail, she guessed. There was no need to guess the type of pipe though. The ting of it let Auri know it was iron, black and twice the thicken of her thumb. The nightjar tapped the pipe again, then dipped down to the pool to drink.

After it drank, the bird winged quickly back to its previous perch. Back to the pipe. Back to stand in the center of the dim grey light. It tapped a third and final time.

Auri's gut went cold. She sat up straight and eyed the bird intently. It stared back at her for a long moment, then flew away, having done what it had come to do.

She looked after it numbly, the chill in her gut making a slow knot. She couldn't ask for things to be more clear than that. Her pulse began to hammer at her then, her palms all sudden sweat.

She took off running and was gone a dozen steps before she remembered herself and hurried back. Embarrassed at her rudeness, she gave the brazen gear a kiss so it would know she wasn't leaving it. She would be back. Then she turned and sprinted off.

First to Mantle, where she washed her face and hands and feet. She took a handkerchief out of her cedar box and pelted down through Rubric and Downings to Borough. Breathing hard, she finally stood before the unassuming wooden door that led to Tenance.

Her gut all sour and chill with fear, Auri looked around the edges of the door and relaxed to see faint cobweb there. There was still time. Perhaps. She pressed her ear against the wood and listened a long moment. Nothing. She slowly pulled it open.

Standing anxious in the doorway, Auri peered into the dusty room. She eyed the cobwebs hanging from the ceiling, she eyed the tables strewn with dusty tools. She eyed the shelves, packed with bottles, boxes, tin containers. She eyed the other door across the room. There was no hint of light around its edges.

Auri did not like it here. It was not the Underthing. This was a between place. It was not for her. But as much as she did not like it, the other options were all worse.

She eyed the floor, covered with a fine layer of dust except for a set of heavy bootprints, black smudges scuffing through the grey dust on the floor. The bootprints told a story. They entered from the other door, moved from a table to a nearby shelf, then made a line to the doorway where she stood.

Auri glared at the spot where they crossed the threshold. As they left the dusty floor of Tenance the bootprints became invisible. They were from long ago. But even now the sight made her heart thump. Her skin was all hot prickle, indignant at the thought of them. A second set of bootprints told the story in reverse. They returned to Tenance from the Underthing. They moved to tables, shelf, and out the other door. They made a circle of sorts. A circuit.

They were not new bootprints. Still, they told a story Auri did not love. They told a story she did not want to see repeated.

She drew a breath to calm herself. There was no time for this. They would be coming, all hard boots and arrogance and not one bit of proper knowledge of this place. A cold sweat swept the prickle heat all off her skin. She drew another calming breath and focused.

Her expression fierce, Auri took a deep breath and crossed the threshold into Tenance. She placed her small white foot inside the black print of a boot. Her foot was small enough that this was no hard thing. Even so, she moved with slow deliberation. Her second step brought little more than her toes in contact with the floor. Her feet fit easily inside the bootprints, making no marks of their own.

Thus she moved, one delicate step at a time. First to a shelf, she eyed containers before picking up a heavy bottle with a ground glass stopper. Next she took a brush and felt the bristles with her finger. Then she made her way back to the door, her steps as slow and graceful as a fawn's.

She closed the door behind her. Then, breathing out a sigh of deep relief, she ran herself to Rubric.

Even moving quickly, it took an hour to find the proper place. Rubric's round brick tunnels ran the length and breadth of Underthing, miles and miles of passages, twisting up and down and doubling back, taking the pipes where they needed to go.

Just as she was fearing she might never find it, just when she'd begun to fear it might not be in Rubric after all, Auri heard a sound like angry snakes and rain. If not for that, it might have taken her all day to track it down. She followed the noise until she could smell damp upon the air.

Finally, turning a corner, she saw water bursting like a fountain from a cracked iron pipe. The spray had wet the bricks for twenty feet in each direction, and the other pipes were dripping with it too. The tiny brass pipes for pressed air didn't mind in the least. And the fat black pisspipe thought the whole thing rather funny. But the steampipe was not best pleased. Its thick wrapping was soaked straight through, and it was grumbling and steaming, filling the tunnel with a musty hothouse damp.

From where she stood, Auri eyed the dark line of the broken black iron pipe, carefully tracing it through the others. Foxen held high, she walked away from the leak, following the dark pipe backward.

After ten minutes and a quick detour through Tenners, Auri found the valve, a small wheel barely big enough for both her hands. Setting down her brush and bottle, she gripped it tight and twisted. Nothing. So she brought the handkerchief out of her pocket, wrapped it round the wheel, and tried again, her teeth bared with the effort. After a long moment, the ungreased age of it gave way, and it grudgingly let itself be spun.

She gathered up her tools and headed back. There was no sound of snakes. The spray had stopped, but the entire tunnel was still sodden. The air hung wet and heavy, making her hair stick and cling to her face.

Auri sighed. It was just as Master Mandrag said so many years ago. She walked back where the tunnel floor was dry and sat cross-legged on the bricks among the pipes.

Then came the hardest part. The waiting grit at her. She had so much to do. This was important, certainly. But he was coming on the seventh day, and she was nowhere near to ready. . . .

She heard something in the distance. Some echo of a sound. A scuff? A step? The sound of boots? Auri went startled and still. She closed her hand over Foxen and sat all quiet in the sudden dark, straining to hear. . . .

But no. There was nothing. The Underthing was host to a thousand small moving things, water in pipes, wind through Billows, the rumbling thrum of wagons filtering through the cobblestones, half-heard voices echoing down the grates. But no boots. Not now. Not yet.

She uncovered Foxen and went to look at the leak again. The air was still hot and thick with wet, so she went back to her sitting place where there was nothing to do but fidget and worry. Auri considered running back to fetch the brazen gear. Then at least she would have company. But no. She had to stay.

A leak was bad. But a leak might go unnoticed for some time. Now, with the water to this piece of pipe turned off entire, there was every chance that something vital up above was all alack. No knowing what. The pipe could lead to some disused piece of Mains, where it could stay dry for years with no one anyways the wiser.

But perhaps it led to the Master's Hall, and right now one of them was halfway through a bath. What if it led to Crucible, and some experiment left to calmly calcinate was instead undergoing unintended exothermic full cascade?

It led to the same thing. Upset. Folk finding keys. Folk opening doors. Strangers in her Underthing, shining their unseemly lights about. Their smoke. The braying of their voices. Tromping everywhere with hard, uncaring boots. Looking at everything without a single thought of what a look entails. Poking things and messing them about without the slightest sense of what was proper.

Auri realized her fists were knots of knuckle white. She shook herself and stood. Her hair hung lank around her head.

The air was clearer now. Not wet and steaming any more. She gathered up her tools and was glad to see the steampipe had finally roasted both itself and everything around it dry. Better still, the slow regard of silent things had wafted off the moisture in the air.

Auri brought Foxen close to the black iron pipe, and was relieved to see the trouble was no greater than a hair-thin crack. Though the pipe looked dry, she wiped it with her handkerchief. Wiped it again. Then she unstoppered the bottle, dipped her brush, and spread clear liquid all across the tiny break.

Wrinkling her nose at the knifelike smell, Auri dipped her brush again, painting all around the pipe. She grinned and eyed the bottle. It was lovely. Tenaculum was tricky stuff, but this was perfect. Not thick like jam, not thin like water. It clung and stuck and spread. It was full of green grass and leaping and . . . sulphonium? Naphtha? Hardly what she would have used, but you couldn't argue with results. The craft employed was undeniable.

Soon she had coated the entire pipe around the crack in glistening liquid. She licked her lips, looked up, then worked her mouth and spat delicately onto the far edge of the wet. The surface of the tenaculum rippled and her grin grew wider. She reached out a finger and was pleased to find it hard and smooth as glass. Oh yes. Whoever wrought and factored this was living proof that alchemy was art. It showed pure mastery of craft.

Auri painted two more coats, laving all way round the pipe and for a handspan off beside the hairline crack. Twice more she spat to set and glaze it. Then she stoppered up the bottle, kissed it, smiled, and sprinted back to turn the water on.

Her duty done, Auri tended to the brush and headed back to Tenance. She pressed her ear against the door. Listened. She heard a faint . . . No. Nothing. She held her breath and listened. Nothing.

Even so, she opened the door slowly. She looked inside to see there was no light around the other door. For a moment her heart stuttered as she thought she saw new bootprints on . . . But no. Just shadow. Just her own breath-catching fear.

Carefully she put the bottle back upon its shelf, setting it inside its own dark dustless ring where she had found it. And then the brush. She stepped carefully inside the big black brutish treadings of the boots. She wasn't one for rucking things about. She stepped the way the water moves within a gentle wave. Never mind the motion, the water stays unchanged. That was the proper way of things.

She slowly closed the heavy door behind her. She checked the latch to make herself most certain sure. Stepping back into the Underthing, the stones should have been sweet beneath her feet. But they were not. They were mere stones. The air seemed strange and strained. Something was wrong.

She stopped and listened at the door again. She listened closer, then opened up the door a crack to peer inside. Nothing. She closed the door and checked the latch. She leaned her weight against the door and tried to sigh but could not find the breath for it inside her chest. Something was wrong. She had forgotten something.

Auri ran back to Rubric, heart stuttering as she turned wrong. Then wrong again. But then she found the valve again. She went down on her knees to make herself most certain sure she'd turned it open and not closed. She put both hands upon the pipe and felt the tremble of the water running through.

Not that then. But still. Had she moved carefully enough? Had she left a smudge upon the floor? Auri sprinted back to Tenance and put her ear against the door. Nothing. She opened the door and lifted Foxen high so that his light shone down onto the dust. Nothing.

By now her skin was all asheen with sweat. She closed the heavy door. She checked the latch and leaned her slender weight against it, pressing with her hands and forehead. She tried to breathe more deeply but her heart was stiff and tight inside her chest. There was something wrong about the air. The door refused to sit right in its frame. She pressed against it with both palms. She checked the latch. Foxen's light seemed suddenly too thin. Had she moved carefully enough? No. She knew. She listened, then opened up the door and looked again. Nothing. But simply seeing did not help. She knew that seeming wasn't hardly half of things. Something was wrong. She tried, but she could simply not unclench. She could not catch her breath. The stones beneath her feet were nothing like her stones. She needed to get somewhere safe.

Despite the stones, the strangeness in the air, Auri started walking back to Mantle. She took the safest way, but even so her steps were slow. And even so, she sometimes had to stop and close her eyes and merely breathe. And even so, the breathing hardly helped. How could it when the air itself had gone untrue?

The angles were all wrong in Pickering but she didn't realize how lost she had become until she looked around and found herself in Scaperling. She did not know how she had come to be so out of place, but there was no denying where she was. The damp was all around.

The smell of rot. The grit under her feet. The way the walls were leering. She turned and turned again but could not find her place.

She tried to push ahead. She knew that if she walked and turned and walked eventually she must leave grim, gritty Scaperling behind. She would come out into a friendly place. Or at least a place that did not twist and cramp and loom all round her.

So she walked and turned and looked around, hoping beyond hope for a glimpse of the familiar. Hoping that the stones might slowly start to belong underneath her feet. But no. The hammer of her heart told her to run. She needed her safe place. She needed to get back to Mantle. But where was the way of it? Even if she knew the way, the air was growing tight and dizzy all around her. Though she was loath to touch them, Auri stretched her hand to lean against the sharp unkindness of the wall.

Slow steps. A turn. She smiled to see things open up ahead of her. Finally. Her chest began to loosen up when finally she saw the end of Scaperling ahead. She took two steps before she realized what way it offered out. She stopped. No. No no. The tangle of unwelcome tunnel opened up ahead. But it opened out into the vast and empty quiet of Black Door.

Auri did not even turn around. She merely took step after slow and sliding step back the same way she had come. It was hard. The wall caught at her hand and worried it, scraping skin off of her knuckles. The damp tight knot of Scaperling did not want her back inside. But Black Door did. The wide and welcome path to Black Door stretched before her like a dark black open mouth. A maw. A maul.

Step after step she forced her way backward into Scaperling. She did not dare to let the way to Black Door out of sight. She did not dare let it behind her, all unseen. Unseemly. All unseamed.

Finally she backed around a corner and sank trembling to the floor. She needed everything to not come all apart around her. She needed to get back to Mantle. She needed her most perfect place. There the stones were safe under her feet. There everything was sweet and proper true.

She was dizzy and askant and slant. She shook and could not bring herself to stand, so she folded herself in and sat crosslegged upon the floor.

She sat there for a long and silent while. She closed her eyes. She closed her mouth. She covered Foxen with her hand. All small she sat. All still. The grubby dank of Scaperling got in her hair, made it hang heavy. She let her tangleness fall all around her in a curtain. It made a tiny space inside. It was a small space just for her.

Auri opened up her eyes and looked into this tiny private place. She saw brave Foxen bravely shining in the shelter of her hands. She uncovered him, and even though his light was thin and thready, the sight of him in this small space made Auri smile. She felt around inside herself for her true perfect name and though it took a long and lonesome moment, finally she felt it there. It was shivery and scant. Scared. Skint. But just around the edges it was still scintillant. It was still hers. It shone.

Moving slowly, Auri stood and made her slow way out of Scaperling. The air was thick and shuddersome. The walls were full of spite. The stones begrudged her every step. All everything was snarling allapart. But even so she found her way to Pickering, the walls were merely sullen there. Then she made her way to Dunnings.

Then Auri finally felt the stones of Mantle underneath her feet. She lightly stepped inside her oh most perfect place. She washed her face and hands and feet. It helped. She sat for a long moment in her perfect chair. She enjoyed her perfect leaf. She breathed the lovely ordinary air. Her skin no longer felt stretched tight. Her heart grew buttery and warm. Foxen was fulsome again, even effulgent.

Auri went to Van and brushed her hair until the damp and tangle were all gone. She drew a breath and sighed it out. Her name was sweet inside her chest. All things were in their proper place again. She grinned.

BEAUTIFUL AND BROKEN

AFTER TAKING A MOMENT for her leisure, Auri got a drink of water from the pool in Mote, then headed back down to gather up the brazen gear. It was patient as three stones, but still, it deserved to find its proper place as much as anyone.

For lack of any better ideas, Auri carried it down to Wains. Perhaps it belonged there. Or better yet, perhaps the brazen thing might hint to her of what the tiny hidden wrongness was that kept the sitting room from ringing sweetly as a bell.

Or perhaps she might see the gear in a better light down there. Especially with the place so new and nearly perfect. It was as good a place as any, she supposed.

So down she went, to proper, rich, wood-paneled Wains. Then into her new sitting room. She sat the brazen gear upon the couch and curled up close beside it, tucking her feet underneath herself.

It wasn't any more content. Auri sighed and cocked her head at it. Poor thing. To be so lovely and so lost. To be all answerful with all that knowing trapped inside. To be beautiful and broken. Auri nodded and lay her hand gently on the gear's smooth face consolingly.

Perhaps Throughbottom? Why hadn't she thought of that before? True, when she thought of love and answers, the ancient wreckage in the cavern hardly sprang to mind. But maybe that was just the point. Perhaps some long-dead hulking mechanata was in desperate need of nine bright teeth and love in its abandoned heart?

Auri ran one finger down its side, her skin snagging a little on the jagged edge where its tenth tooth was torn away.

That's when it struck her like a thunderclap. She knew exactly what was wrong. Of course. She leapt up to her feet, grinning excitedly. She pulled the corner of the carpet up, rolling it until she saw the button laying there, content.

Her hands flew to her pockets, looking for . . . Yes.

Auri set the tarnished buckle down beside the button. She nudged it closer. Turned it. There. She trembled slightly as she put the carpet back in place. She smoothed it flat with both her hands.

She came to her feet and there was a click inside her

like a key inside a lock. The room was perfect as a circle now. Like a bell. Like the moon when it was perfect full.

Auri laughed in delight, and every piece of the laughing was a tiny bird come tumbling out to fly around the room.

She stood in the center of the room and spun in a circle to see it all. And when her eyes passed over the ring on the table, she saw it no longer belonged here. It was free to go as it pleased. It sang golden all through itself, and the amber it held was gentle as an autumn afternoon.

Brimming with joy, Auri danced. Her bare feet white against the moss-soft darkness of the carpet.

•••◦◉◦•••

Her heart tumbling happily within her, Auri gathered up the brazen gear again, smiling as her hands closed around it. She was barely halfway back to Mantle when she heard a hint of music.

Auri went as motionless as stone. Silent as the stillness in a heart. It couldn't be. Not yet. She had days and days. She wasn't nearly—

She heard again. Faint. A sound that could have been the chime of glass on glass, that might have been a bird, but that might also be the distant singing of a tight-stretched string.

He was here! Days early and her half-smudged and empty-handed both. But even so, her heart stepped sideways in her chest at the thought of seeing him again.

Auri sprinted back to Mantle faster than a rabbit with a wolf behind. She took the fastest way, even though it went through Faceling with its damp and fear and the horrid smell of hot flowers hanging in the air.

Back in Mantle, she set the brass gear up above the fireplace. Then Auri washed her face and hands and feet. She shucked herself and donned her favorite dress.

Then, quivering with nervous excitement, she hurried into Port and eyed the shelves. Not the bone, of course. Not the book either. Not yet. She put two fingers on the crystal, picked it up, turned it over. She breathed, tasting the air. She put it down again.

She shifted foot to foot and glanced into Mantle. Her perfect yellow leaf was almost right. The brazen gear was sullen now, and much too proud. He had enough of that.

There was her newfound ring of autumn gold. That was fine enough, surely. And it suited him, twice bright. But as a gift it was . . . foreboding. She did not wish to hint at him of demons.

Then she spied the small jar, mouth open. Her eyes flicked over to the other shelf with its scattering of holly berry, bright as blood upon the cloth. Excitement welled up in her chest. She grinned.

She grabbed the berries and funneled them into the tiny bottle. They fit perfectly. Of course. They were dutiful and true. Hollybottle. To keep him safe. An early visit. Music.

It was more makeshift than she liked. Barely proper.

But truth be told *he* was the early one. It was sufficient for an early visit. She darted out the door, her feet tap tapping all the way through Grimsby, then down Oars, and finally up to Trip Beneath.

Auri paused there, underneath the heavy drainage grate. Her heart hammered as she tried to listen. Nothing. Had she really heard? Was he waiting? Had she dithered until he had grown bored and left?

She put Foxen in his tiny box, then worked the hidden catch and pushed against the heavy iron bars above with trembling arms. The grate swung wide, and Auri clambered up to Applecourt, sheltered by the hedges there. She went still. Listened. No voices. Good. No light in the windows. Good.

The moon was looking into Applecourt. Not a good moon. Auri looked out from the safety of the hedge, peering at the sky. No clouds. She closed her eyes and listened again. Nothing.

She took a deep breath and darted through the open grass to stand beneath the sheltering branches of Lady Larbor. There she stopped to breathe, going still as steading. After looking round again, she scampered up the twisty branches. It was tricky with the hollybottle in one hand. She slipped a little, rough bark scritching at the bottoms of her feet.

Then she was On Top Of Things. She could see everything and forever. All of Temerant spooled endlessly away beneath her feet. It was so nice she almost didn't care about the moon.

She could see the prickly chimbleys of Crucible, and winged Mews all full of flickerlight. To the east she spied the silver line of the Old Stone Road cutting gully-deep into the forest, off to Stonebridge, over the river, and away away away. . . .

But he wasn't here. There wasn't anything. Just warm tar under her feet. And chimbleys. And the sharpness of the moon.

Auri clutched the hollybottle in her hand. She looked around and stepped into the shadow of a brick-tree chimbley so the moon couldn't watch her.

She held her breath and listened. He wasn't here. But maybe. Maybe if she waited.

She looked around. The wind huffed by and swirled her hair around her face. She brushed it back, frowning. He wasn't here. Of course he wasn't. He wasn't coming till the seventh day. She knew. She knew the way of things.

Auri stood there motionless, her hands close to her chest. She held the hollybottle. Her eyes flicked about the moonswept rooftops.

She sat cross-legged on the tin, in the shadow of brickery.

She looked around. She waited.

A QUITE UNCOMMON
PLEASANT PLACE

EVENTUALLY A CLOUD hid the moon. Smug thing. And Auri took the chance to scamper back into the Underthing.

Her heart was heavy all the way through Tenners. But she found a large tangle of dry wood in Umbrel, washed down the grates in some forgotten storm. Ash and elm and hawthorn. So much wood it took six trips to carry all of it to Mantle. It was quite a find, and by the end of it, she was near to whistling.

Auri washed her face and hands and feet. Smiling at the smell of her yet-more-slender sliver of sweet soap, she donned her second favorite dress again. It was still a doing day.

After filling her pockets and picking up her gathersack, she made her way to Mandril. She didn't even need to wet her feet, as there hadn't been a heavy rain in ages. At the farthest tail of the twisting way, Auri stopped before the final corner. There was a hint of moonlight up ahead, so she gave Foxen a quick kiss before tucking him inside his tiny wooden box.

She took the final piece of Mandril more by memory than sight, stepping carefully until she stood behind the upright runoff grate that looked out onto nothing much except the bottom of a gully. Auri moved to stand next to the heavy bars. From there she saw the bulk of Haven up upon the hill, a shadow looming large against the starry sky. A few lights burned in windows, some red, some yellow, and one up on the topmost floor a bright and chilling blue.

She held her breath then. No voices. No hooves. No howling. She looked up and saw the stars, the moon, and a few slender shreds of cloud. She watched the cloudscrap slowly scull across the sky. She waited till it hid the slender moon.

Only then did Auri work the hidden latch inside the grate so it swung open like a door. Then she scurried up the gully, across a stretch of well-groomed lawn, and ducked into the shadows underneath a spreading oak.

She stood there, motionless a while until her heart stopped racing. Until she was most certain sure that she had not been seen.

Then Auri edged around the tree until the building could no longer see her. And after that she turned and disappeared into the woods.

⊶⟐⟐⊷

Auri found the place while picking pine cones. A small, forgotten graveyard, stones overgrown with ivy. Roses ran wild, climbing the remains of an ancient wrought-iron fence.

Arms close to her body, hands beneath her chin, Auri stepped into the graveyard. Her tiny feet were silent as she moved among the stones.

The moon was out again, but she was lower now, and bashful. Auri smiled at her, glad for the company now that she was no longer On Top of Things and Haven was far gone behind. Here on the edge of the clearing the moon showed acorns scattered on the ground. Auri spent a few minutes picking up the ones with perfect hats and tucking them into her gathersack.

She strolled between the stones, stopping at a broken

one, the letters worn away with rain and age. She touched it with two fingers and moved on. She lifted up the ivy on a monument, then turned to see the laurel tree that loomed in the far corner of the yard. Its roots were all among the stones, its branches spread above. It was a lonely thing. All odd and out of place.

Stepping close, her small feet fitting neatly in between the roots, Auri pressed her hand against the tree's dark trunk. She breathed in deep the warm scent of its leaves. She slowly circled it and spied a dark gap down among the roots.

Nodding, Auri reached into her gathersack and brought out the bone that she had found the day before. She bent down and tucked it deep inside the dark and hollow space beneath the tree. She smiled with satisfaction.

Standing, she dusted off her knees and stretched. Then she began to pick the small blue laurel fruit and put them in her gathersack as well.

•••◦◉◦•••

She explored the forest after that. She found a mushroom, which she ate. She found a leaf and breathed on it. She looked up at the stars.

Later still, Auri crossed a creek she'd never seen before and was surprised to find a tiny farmhouse tucked among the trees.

Surprised but pleased. It was a seemly place. All stone, with slate upon its pointed roof. On the back porch, near the door, there was a small table. A wooden plate covered with an overturned wooden bowl rested there. Beside it was a bowl of clay, covered with a glazed clay plate.

Auri lifted the wooden bowl and found a piece of fresh brown bread beneath. It held health and heart and hearth. A lovely thing, and full of invitation. She put it in her pocket.

She knew the other bowl held milk, but the plate that covered it faced up. It was not for her. She left it for the faeries.

Keeping in the shadow, Auri made her way around the garden to the barn. There was a strange dog there, all gristle and bay. It massed half again as much as her, its shoulders coming nearly to her chest. It stepped out of the shadows when she came close to the barn.

It was black, with a thick neck and scars all cross its face. One ear was ragged and chewed from some forgotten fight. It padded closer to her, massive head held low, moving suspiciously from side to side, eyeing her.

Auri grinned and held out her hand. The dog snuffled at her, then licked her fingers before making a great gawp of a yawn and settling down to sleep.

The barn was huge: stone below with painted wood above. The doors were closed and fastened with a fat iron paddock lock. But high above, the hayloft was thrown wide to greet the night. Auri climbed the ivy-knotted stone as quickly as a squirrel. She went slower up the second half, the barn-boards odd against her fingers and her feet.

The barn was full of musk and sleep. Dark too, save for a few thin bands of moonlight slanting through the wooden walls. Auri opened Foxen's tiny box, and his blue-green light welled out to fill the open space.

An old horse nuzzled Auri's neck as she walked by his stall. She smiled at him and took the time to brush his tail and mane. There was a pregnant nanny goat which bleated out a greeting. Auri scooped some grain into her trough. There was a cat, and they ignored each other.

Auri spent some time there, looking over everything. The grindstone. The quern. The small, well-fitted churn. A bearskin stretched upon a rack to cure. It was a quite uncommon, pleasant place. Everything was tended to and loved. Nothing she could see was useless, lost, or wrong.

Well, *nearly* nothing. Even the tightest ship lets slip a little water. A single turnip had gone tumbling from its bin to lie abandoned on the floor. Auri put it in her gathersack.

There was a large stone sweatbox, too. It was stacked with slabs of ice, each thicker than a cinder brick and twice as long. Inside she found butchered meat and sweet cream butter. There was a lump of suet in a bowl, a sheet of honeycomb upon a tray.

The suet was enraged. It was a storm of autumn apples, age, and anger. It wanted nothing more than to be on its way. She tucked it deep inside her bag.

Oh. But the honeycomb. It was lovely. Not one bit stolen. The farmer loved the bees and did things in the proper way. It was full of silent bells and drowsy summer afternoon.

Auri felt inside her pockets. Her fingers passed over the crystal and the small stone doll. The rock wasn't proper for this place either. She reached inside her gathersack and felt around among the acorns she'd collected.

For a long moment, it seemed like nothing she had

brought would make a proper fit. But then her fingers found it and she knew. Carefully she brought out the length of fine white tatted lace. She folded it and left it near the churn. It was the careful work of many long and drowsy autumn days. It would find purpose in a place like this.

Then Auri took the clean white cloth that had held the hollyberry earlier and rubbed it with some butter. Then she broke off a piece of sticky comb the size of her spread hand and wrapped it up as tidy as can be.

She would have loved to have some butter too, as hers was full of knives. There were eleven squared-off pats of it lined up upon the sweatbox shelf. Full of clover and birdsong and, oddly, sullen hints of clay. Even so they were all lovely. Auri searched her gathersack and looked through all her pockets twice, but in the end she still came up alack.

She closed the sweatbox tight. Then up the ladder to the open window of the loft. She put Foxen away, then made her slow way down the side of the barn, gathersack slung tight across her back.

On the ground Auri brushed her floating hair out of her face, then kissed the hulking dog atop his sleeping head. She skipped around the corner of the barn and took a dozen steps before the prickle on her neck told her that she was being watched.

She froze mid-step, gone still as stone. Touched by the wind, her hair moved of its own accord, slowly drifting to surround her face as gently as a puff of smoke.

Moving nothing but her eyes, Auri saw her. Up on the second floor, in the blackness of an open window, Auri saw a pale face even smaller than her own. A little girl was watching her, eyes wide, a tiny hand against her mouth.

What had she seen? Foxen's green light shining through the slats? Auri's tiny shape, obscured by hair like thistlepuff, barefoot in the moonlight?

Auri's sudden smile was hidden by the curtain of her hair. She did a cartwheel then. Her first in ages. Her fine hair following, a comet tail. She cast her eyes around and saw a tree, a dark hole in its trunk. Auri danced toward it, twirling and leaping, then bent to look inside the hole.

Then, her back to the farmhouse, Auri opened Foxen's box and heard a single tiny gasp thread through the silent night behind her. She pressed one hand against her mouth so that she wouldn't laugh. The hole was perfect, just deep enough so that a little girl could reach inside and feel around. If she were curious, that is.

If she were brave enough to stick her arm in nearly to her shoulder.

Auri pulled the crystal from her pocket. She kissed it, brave explorer that it was, and lucky too. It was the perfect thing. This was the perfect place. True, she was no longer in the Underthing. But even so, this was so true it could not be denied.

She wrapped the crystal in a leaf and lay it in the bottom of the hole.

Then she ran into the trees, dancing, leaping, giggling high and wild.

••➤➤◗➤➤••

She went back to the boneyard then, and climbed atop a large flat slab. Back straight and smiling, Auri made a proper dinner for herself of soft brown bread with just a hint of honey. For afters she had pine nuts fresh-picked from their cones, each one a tiny, perfect treat.

All the while her heart was brimming. Her grin was brighter than the slender crescent moon. She licked her fingers too, as if she were some tawdry thing, all wicked and unseemly.

HOLLOW

ON THE THIRD DAY, Auri wept.

THE ANGRY DARK

WHEN AURI WOKE on the fourth day, things had changed.

She could tell before she stretched awake. Before she cracked her eyes into the seamless dark. Foxen was frightened and full of mountains. So today was a tapering day. A burning day.

She didn't blame him. She knew what it could be like. Some days simply lay on you like stones. Some were fickle as cats, sliding away when you needed comfort, then coming back later when you didn't want them, jostling at you, stealing your breath.

No. She didn't blame Foxen. But for half a minute she wished it was a different sort of day, even though she knew that nothing good could come from wanting at the world. Even though she knew it was a wicked thing to do.

Even so, burning days were flickersome. Too frangible by half. They were not good days for doing. They were good days for staying put and keeping the ground steady underneath your feet.

But she only had three days left. There was still so much to do.

Moving gently in the dark, Auri picked up Foxen from his dish. He fairly smoldered with fear, there would be no persuading him like this, so sullen he was nearly truculent. So she gave him a kiss and returned him to his proper place. Then she made her way out of bed under the tenebrific blanket of the full and heavy dark. It made no difference if her eyes were open, so she left them closed while her hands sought out her cedar box. She left them closed while she brought out matches and a candle.

She dragged a match against the floor where it spittered, sparked, then broke. Her heart sank. A bad start for a bad day. The second match hardly sparked at all, just gritted. The third snapped. The fourth flared and faded. The fifth ground itself down into nothing. And that was all of them.

Auri sat for a moment in the dark. It had been like this before sometimes. Not for a long time now, but she remembered. She had been sitting like this, empty as eggshell. Hollow and chest-heavy in the angry dark when she'd first heard him playing. Back before he'd given her her sweet new perfect name. A piece of sun that never left her. It was a bite of bread. A flower in her heart.

Thinking of this made it easier for her to stand. She knew the way to her bedtable. The basin had fresh water. She would wash her face and hands—

But there was no soap. She'd used the last of it. And all her other cakes were off where they belonged, in Bakery.

She sat down on the floor again beside her bed. She closed her eyes. She almost stayed there, too, all cut-string and tangle-haired and lonely as a button.

But he was coming. He would be here soon, all sweet and brave and shattered and kind. He would come carrying and clever-fingered and oh so unaware of oh so many things. He was rough against the world, but even so. . . .

Three days. He would come visiting in three short days. And for all her work and wander, she hadn't found a proper present for him yet. For all that she was wise about the way of things, she hadn't caught an empty echo of anything that she could bring.

No proper gift nor nothing yet to share. It simply wouldn't do. So Auri gathered herself in and climbed up slowly to her feet.

There were three ways out of Mantle. The hallway was dark. The doorway was dark. The door was dark and closed and empty and nothing.

So, without friends or light to guide her, Auri made her slow and careful way out through the hallway, trekking toward Tree.

She went through Candlebear, her fingers brushing the wall lightly so she could find her way. She took the long way round, as Vaults was far too dangerous without a light. Then halfway through Pickering she stopped and turned around for fear that she would find The Black Twelve ahead. The air above as dark and still and chill as the pool below. She could not bear the thought of that today.

That meant there was no way for her but damp and moldy Scaperling instead. And if that weren't enough, the only proper way through Dunnings was unnecessarily narrow and all athwart with webs. They got in her hair, which made her sticky and cross.

But eventually she found her way to Tree. The tiny tickling sound of running water in the cold well came to greet her, and it was only then that she remembered how hungry she was. She found her few remaining matches on the shelf and lit her spirit lamp. The sudden brightness of it hurt her eyes, and even after she recovered, the yellow jumping flame made everything look strange and anxious.

She put the five remaining matches in her pocket and took a drink of water from the cold well. The shelves looked more empty than usual in the odd, jittery light. She rinsed her hands and face and feet in the icy water. Then she sat down on the floor and ate the turnip in small bites. Then she ate her last remaining fig. Her tiny face was grave. The smell of nutmeg prickled in the air.

•••◗◗●◖◖•••

All flickerling and sticky with web, Auri made her way to Bakery. It wasn't oveny today. It was hunkered down and sullen, like a forgotten kiln.

She passed the mellow pipes and turned and turned again before she made her way to the little bricky niche so perfect for her hoard of soap to season in. Not hot, but dry. And—

There was no soap. Her soap was gone.

But no. It was the shifting light from the spirit lamp, tricking her. All odd and yellow. It threw shadows everywhere. It changed the Underthing. It couldn't be trusted. This was obviously a different little bricky niche, empty as anything.

She turned around and followed her own footsteps back to Emberling. Then she went back, counting turns. Left and right. Left then left then right.

No. This was Bakery. This was her niche. But there was nothing there. No burlap sack. No careful cakes of perfect summer soap. Even in the low red radiant of that place Auri felt ice in her belly. Was someone in her Underthing? Was someone moving things about? Rucking up the smoothness of all her long, hard years of work?

All watery and loose inside she searched about, peering around corners and shining her lamp into shadows. Barely ten feet away, she found her burlap sack torn to tatters. Underneath the scent of her sweet cinnas soap was the smell of musk and piss. There was a tuft of fur where some small climbing beast had rubbed itself against a jutting brick.

Auri stood. All tangle-haired and sticky. Her tiny face was stunned at first, numb in the flickerling yellow. Then her mouth grew furious. Her eyes went hard. Some *thing* had eaten all her perfect soap.

Reaching out, she took the tuft of fur between her fingers. The gesture was so tight with rage she feared she'd snap and crack the world in two. Eight cakes. An entire winter's worth of soap. Some thing had eaten all the perfect soap she'd made. It dared come here, into the proper place for soap, and eat it *all*.

She stamped her foot. She hoped the greedy thing shit for a span of days. She hoped it shit its awful self inside-out and backward, then fell into a crack and lost its name and died alone and hollow-empty in the angry dark.

She threw the tuft of fur down on the floor. She tried to run her fingers through her hair, but they snagged up in her tangleness. For a second her hard eyes went all brimful, but she blinked them back.

Hot from Bakery, and all asweat with rage and the

unrightness of it all, Auri turned and stormed away, her bare feet slapping angrily against the stone.

•••◗◗••

Heading back to Mantle, Auri took the shorter way. All draggled and smirched she took a moment to dunk herself in the pool at the bottom of The Silver Twelve and felt a little better for it. It was no kind of proper bath. A dip. A rinse. And chilly. But better than nothing, if only just. The moon peered faintly through the grate above. But she was kind and distant, so Auri didn't mind.

Getting out of the water, she shook herself and rubbed her damp skin with her hands. She couldn't think of going back to Bakery to dry. Not today. She eyed the moonlight peering in the grates above and had just begun to squeeze the water from her hair when she heard it. A tiny splashing. A tiny mewling squeak. The sound of distress.

She dashed around in a long moment of panic. Sometimes a lost thing found its way down to the bottom of The Twelve and fell into the pool while drinking.

It took a breathless time to find it. Her damned awful flickerlight seemed to shed more shadow than it burned away. And echoes came from everywhere, scattered by the pipes and water in The Silver Twelve, so ears were hardly any help at all.

Finally she found it. A tiny thing, mewling and paddling weakly. It was the next thing to a baby, barely old enough to be out on its own. Auri took hold of a hanging brace and leaned out long across the water, one leg lifting up for balance while her other arm went out above her head. She stretched like a dancer. Her hand described a gentle arc and dipped into the pool, gently scooping the tiny draggled thing up. . . .

And it *bit* her. It sunk its teeth into the meaty bit between her finger and her thumb.

Auri blinked and pulled herself back to the edge, cupping the small skunk gently in her hand. It struggled, and she was forced to grip it tighter than she liked. If it fell into the pool again, it might gasp and drown before she found and fetched it out.

Once both her feet were back upon the stone, Auri made a cage for the tiny skunk with both her hands against her chest. With no hands left to hold her lamp, Auri trusted to the moonlight as she scurried up Old Ironways. It squirmed and scratched at her chest, fighting to be free, biting her a second time on the tip-pad of her smallest finger.

But by then she'd reached the nearest grate. She lifted up her hand and nudged the poor lost thing outside. Out of the Underthing and back toward its proper nighttime place of mothers, bins, and cobblestones.

Auri made her way back to the bottom of The Silver Twelve and ducked her throbbing hand into the pool. It stung quite badly, but truthfully, it was her feelings that were worst hurt. It had been a mortal age since anything had been so rude to her.

Her name hung dark and heavy in her chest as Auri dragged her dress on over her head. It didn't fit her properly today. It felt like everything was leering at her in the yellow light. Her hair was dreadful.

Auri walked back to Mantle, taking the long way around to avoid Van so she wouldn't have to see herself in her mirror. Coming into Port, she saw that nearly everything was wrong. Of course. It was just that sort of day.

She set the lamp on the table harder than she needed to, making the flame jump high. Then she did her best to set the place to rights. Hollybottle close beside the folded secrets of the all uncut octavo book? No. By itself on the farthest edge of secondshelf. The resin wanted its own space. The brimful jar of dark blue laurel fruit moved back onto the corner table. The tiny stone figurine perched high upon the wine rack, as if it were so much better than the rest of them.

The only thing that kept its place was her new-won perfect piece of honeycomb. She almost took a bite of it for no good reason other than to brighten up her day. She might have too, selfish as that would be. But she couldn't bear the thought of touching it, given the state that she was in.

When things were squared away as well as she could

manage, Auri took the lamp and stepped through, into Mantle. Her cedar box was in a state of minor disarray, and there were broken matches strewn about, but both of those were quickly mended. The brazen gear was fine. Her perfect leaf. Her box of stone. Her ring of autumn gold. Her grey glass bottle filled with lavender. All fine. She felt herself relax a bit.

Then she saw her blanket. Her perfect blanket she had made herself in only the most proper way. It had twisted and the corner lay all naked on the floor.

Auri merely stood there for a long moment. She

thought that she might cry, but when she felt around inside herself she found she had no crying left. She was full of broken glass and burrs. She was weary and disappointed with all of everything. And her hand hurt.

But there was no crying left in her. So instead she gathered up her blanket and carried it to Billows. After searching out a clean brass pipe, she hung it like a curtain in the center of the tunnel, let the endless wind brush past, and watched it wicker gently back and forth. It billowed and luffed, but that was all.

Auri frowned and moved to pull the blanket down again. But she was careless, and a puff of wind blew out her lamp. Re-lighting it cost her another precious match.

Once Billows was full of flickerlight again, Auri tugged the blanket down, turned it over, and hung it on the pipe again. But no. Frontways or backways, it didn't make a lick of difference.

Next she climbed Old Ironways and found the grate that loved the moon the most. Her pale light feathered down like snowdrops, like a silver spear. Auri spread the blanket out to catch the moon, to bask in it.

It didn't help.

She carried the blanket backward through the whole of Winnoway. She took it to the top of Draughting, threw it off, and watched it plummet through the maze of wires until it snagged one near the bottom and hung there, bobbing gently up and down. She carried it back to Mantle and wrapped it round the horrid, galling, stubborn brazen gear that stood there gloating and golden in the flickerling light.

None of it did a bit of good.

Unable to think of anywhere else that might help ease the offense, Auri carried the blanket all the way down to Wains and into her new perfect sitting room. She draped it over the back of the couch. She folded it and set it in the chair.

Finally, in true desperation, Auri set her jaw and spread her blanket flat across the lush red rug in the center of the room. She smoothed it with both hands, careful not to let it touch the stone of the floor. It overlapped the rug almost perfectly. And for a second she felt hope rise in her chest that—

But no. It didn't fix things at all. She knew it then. She'd known all along, really. Nothing was going to make the blanket right again.

Scowling, Auri snatched the blanket up, wadded the ungrateful thing into a ball, and headed up the unnamed stair. She felt flat and scraped as an old hide. Dry as paper written on both sides. Even the playful teasing of the new stone stair could stir no breath of joy in her.

She climbed over the debris, through the broken

wall, and into Tumbrel. The room looked different in the yellow flickerling. Full of looming fear and disappointment.

And when her eyes passed over the vanity, she saw it differently. It was not rakish now. In the shifting light she saw it had a sinister bent, and caught a glimpse of what was turning it from true. She could feel the tattered edges of its disarray.

But tanglehaired and sticky, all unwashed and hollow as she was, she was hardly in the proper state for mending. She was in no mood to tend to the ungrateful thing.

Instead Auri knelt before the wardrobe and set the spirit lamp beside her. Her knees were chilly on the stone floor as she pulled open the drawer and looked down at the creamy folded sheets inside.

Auri closed her eyes. She took a long, stiff breath and sighed it out again.

Eyes still closed, she stuffed the blanket hard into the drawer. Then she lay her hand upon the topmost sheet. Yes. This was fair. Even blind she could sense the sweetness of it. Her fingers trailed across the creamy surface. . . .

She heard a tiny frizzling noise and caught the scent of burning hair.

Auri sprang back, scrabbling madly backward on

all fours, away from the vicious spitting yellow flame. Catching hold of her hair, it was cold comfort to see only a few stray strands were charred. Auri stomped back to the wardrobe, snatched her blanket up, and slammed the drawer, too furious to even think of being properly polite.

Then, climbing through the broken wall, Auri stubbed her toes against a jutting block of stone. She didn't drop her lamp, but it was a near thing. Instead she merely cried in pain, staggering to catch her balance.

Auri sat down hard upon the floor, clutching her foot. It was only then she realized she'd dropped her blanket. It was laying on the naked stone beside her. She grit her teeth so hard she feared that they would break.

After a long moment she gathered up her things, trudged back to Port, and stuffed the blanket angrily into the wine rack. Since that's where it belonged now. Since that's the way things had to be.

•••••◆•••••

Auri spent a long time sitting in her thinking chair, glaring at the brazen gear. It was all glimmer and warm honey in the yellow light. She glared at it all the same. As if it were to blame. As if it were the one that made a mess of everything.

Eventually her sulk burned out. Eventually she calmed enough to realize the truth.

You couldn't fight the tide or change the wind. And if there was a storm? Well, a girl should batten down and bail, not run the rigging. How could she help but make a mess of things, the state that she was in?

She'd strayed from the true way of things. First you set yourself to rights. And then your house. And then your corner of the sky. And after that . . .

Well, then she didn't rightly know what happened next. But she hoped that after *that* the world would start to run itself a bit, like a gear-watch proper fit and kissed with oil. That was what she hoped would happen. Because honestly, there were days she felt rubbed raw. She was so tired of being all herself. The only one that tended to the proper turning of the world.

Still, it was sulk or sail. So Auri stood and rinsed her face and hands and feet. There was no soap, of course. It was no kind of proper wash. It didn't make her feel even a little better. But what else could she do?

She brought the lamp to her lips and puffed out the yellow tongue of flame. Darkness flooded in to fill the room, and Auri climbed into her narrow, naked bed.

•••◦◘◦•••

Auri lay in the dark for a long while. She was tired and tangled and hungry and hollow. She was weary in her heart and head. But even so, sleep would not come.

She thought it was the loneliness at first. Or the chill

that kept her gritty-eyed and shifty. Perhaps it was the dull ache of her twice-bit hand. . . .

But no. Those were no less than she deserved. They were not enough to keep her all wide eyed at night. She'd learned to sleep with worse than that. Back in the times before he'd come. Back in the years before she had her sweet new perfect name.

No. She knew what the problem was. She slid out of her bed and brought out one of her few matches. It struck on the first try, and Auri smiled white in the red light of its sulfurious flaring.

She lit the spirit lamp and carried it to Port. Guiltily, she removed her blanket from the wine rack where she'd stuffed it. She smoothed it gently out across the table, murmuring an apology. And she *was* sorry. She knew better. Cruelty never helped the turning of the world.

She folded the blanket carefully then, her hands gentle. She matched the corners and kept it square and true. Then she found the proper place for it upon the bookshelf, and brought the smooth grey stone so that it wouldn't want for company. It would be cold at night, and she would miss it. But it was happy there. Didn't it deserve to be happy? Didn't everything deserve its proper place?

Still, she cried a bit as she tucked the blanket in, settling it on the shelf.

Auri made her way back into Mantle and sat on her

bed. Then she went back to Port to make sure her crying hadn't skewed things all about. But no. She brushed the blanket with her hands, comforting. It was as it should be. It was happy.

Back in Mantle, Auri moved about the bare room, making sure everything was as it should be. Her thinking chair was just so. Her cedar box was flush against the wall. Foxen's dish and dropper jar were resting on the bedshelf. The brazen gear sat in its niche, indifferent to the world.

The fireplace was empty: clean and trim. Her bedside table held her tiny silver cup. Above the fireplace on the mantelpiece sat her perfect yellow leaf. Her small strong box of stone. Her grey glass jar with kind, dried lavender inside. Her ring of sweet, warm autumn gold.

Auri touched each of these, making sure of them. They were everything they ought to be and nothing else. They were fine as fine.

Despite all of this, she felt unsettled. Here, in her most perfect place.

Auri hurried down to Borough, brought back a broom, and set to sweeping Mantle's floor.

It took an hour. Not because of any mess. But Auri swept slowly and carefully. And there was quite a lot of floor. She didn't often think of it, as Mantle hardly needed tending any more. But it *was* a big place.

It was hers, and the place loved her, and she fit here

like a pea in her own perfect pod. But even so, there was a lot of empty floor.

The floor all fresh, Auri returned the broom. On her way back she wandered through Port to check on the blanket. It seemed to be doing well, but she brought the hollybottle over to keep it company too, just in case. It was a terrible thing to be lonely.

She stepped back into Mantle again and set the spirit lamp on her table. She took her three remaining matches out of her pocket and put them on the table too.

As she sat on the edge of her bed, Auri realized what was out of place. She was herself in disarray. She'd seen something in Tumbrel and not tended to it. Auri thought of the three-mirrored vanity and a tickling finger of guilt ran itself along the edge of her heart.

Even so. She was tired down in her bones now. Weary and hurt. Perhaps just this once . . .

Auri frowned and shook her head furiously. She was a wicked thing sometimes. All full of want. As if the shape of the world depended on her mood. As if she were important.

So she stood and made her slow way back to Tumbrel. Down Crumbledon. Through Wains. Through circle-perfect Annulet and up the unnamed stair.

After climbing through the broken wall, Auri looked hard at the vanity in the flickering light. As she did, she could feel her heart rise slightly in her chest.

The shifting light against three mirrors, it made count-less shadows dance across the bottles there.

Stepping closer, Auri watched carefully. She would never have seen this properly without the shifting na-ture of the yellow light. She stepped left, then right, looking at things from both sides. She tilted her head. She went to her knees so that her eyes were level with the surface of the vanity. A sudden, sunny smile spilled all across her face.

Back straight, Auri sat on the edge of the chair in front of the vanity. She tried not to look in the mirrors, knowing how she must appear. An unwashed, red-eyed, tangled mess. Too thin. Too pale. She was no kind of lady. She opened the two drawers instead and stared into them for a moment, letting the yellow light and shadows slide around inside.

After several minutes, Auri nodded to herself. She removed the pair of gloves from the right-hand drawer and set them near the mirror by a pot of rouge. Then Auri pulled the right-hand drawer completely free and switched it with its partner on the left. She sat there for a long moment, moving the two drawers back and forth in their new tracks, a look of intent concentration on her face.

Everything atop was disarray, bottles and baubles strewn about. Despite that, nearly everything was just the way it ought to be. The only exception was the hair-brush, which Auri tucked into the left-hand drawer by the handkerchiefs, and a small golden brooch with two birds in flight, which she hid beneath a folded fan.

After that, the only thing out of place was a delicate blue bottle with a twisted silver stopper. Like many of the other bottles, it was laying on its side. Auri set it upright, but that wasn't right. She tried to tuck it in a drawer, but it didn't fit there, either.

She picked it up, listening to the liquid tinkling inside. She looked around the room uncertainly. She opened the vanity's drawers again, then slid them closed again. There didn't seem to be a place for it.

She shook the bottle idly in her hand and tapped it with her fingernail. The pale blue glass was delicate as eggshell, but dusty. She gave the bottle a good polishing, hoping it might be a little more forthcoming.

When it was clean it gleamed like the heart of some forgotten icy god. Turning it over in her hands, she saw tiny letters etched across the bottom of the glass. They read: *For My Intoxicating Esther.*

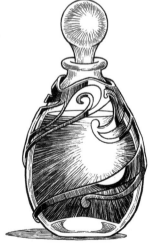

Auri put her hand across her mouth, but a muffled giggle still escaped. Moving slowly, her expression thick with disbelief, she unscrewed the stopper and took a sniff. She laughed openly then, hugely, from deep in her belly. She laughed so hard she could barely screw the top back on. She was still chuckling a minute later as she tucked the bottle deep into her pocket.

She was still smiling when she made her careful way down the unnamed stair and put the bottle carefully away in Port. It liked the bookshelf best, and that was doubly good, as there it would keep both hollybottle and the blanket company.

Auri was still smiling when she climbed into her tiny perfect bed. And yes, it was cold, and lonely too. But that could not be helped. She knew better than anyone, it was worth doing things the proper way.

ASH AND EMBER

WHEN AURI WOKE on the fifth day, Foxen was quite recovered from his mood.

That was for the best. She had a busy lot of work to do.

Laying in the dark, she wondered what the day would bring. Some days were trumpet-proud. They heralded like thunder. Some were courteous, careful as a lettered card upon a silver plate.

But some days were shy. They did not name themselves. They waited for a careful girl to find them.

This was such a day. A day too shy to knock upon her door. Was it a calling day? A sending day? A making day? A mending day?

She could not tell. As soon as Foxen was sufficiently unslumberous, Auri went to Taps and fetched fresh water for her basin. Then back in Mantle she rinsed her face and hands and feet.

There was no soap, of course. That was the very first of things that she would set to rights today. She was not vain enough to work her will against the world. But she could use the things the world had given her. Enough for soap. That was allowed. That was within her rights.

First she lit her spirit lamp. With Foxen's sweet cerulean to soften it, the yellow flame helped warm the room without filling it with frantic shadows clawing at the walls, all jerk and judder.

Auri opened up the flue and set a careful fire with her newfound tangle-wood. So fine and dry. All ash and elm and spry hawthorn. She soon set it crackling to life.

She eyed it for a moment, then turned away. It would be burning for some time. It was just as Master Mandrag always said: nine tenths of chemistry was waiting.

But she had work enough to fill the time. First she ventured down to Tree. She fetched the small copper kettle and her cracked clay cup. She pocketed the empty linen sack. She eyed the butter in the well, then frowned at it and shook her head, knowing better than to borrow trouble with the knives it held.

She lifted out the hard white lump of suet instead, sniffed it curiously and grinned. Then she gathered up the tiny tripod all of iron. She took her sack of salt.

She was just about to leave when she paused and eyed the silver bowl of nutmeg seeds. So strange and rare. So

full of faraway. She picked one up and ran her fingertips along its tippled skin. She brought it to her face and breathed in deep. Musk and thistle. A smell like a bordello curtain, deep and red and full of mysteries.

Still uncertain, Auri closed her eyes and bent her head. The pink tip of her tongue flicked shyly out to touch the strange brown pittem. She stood there, still as still. Then, eyes closed, she brushed the smooth side of it soft across her lips. It was a tender, thoughtful motion. It was nothing like a kiss.

After a long moment, Auri's mouth spread into a wide, delighted smile. Her eyes went wide as lamps. Yes. Yes yes. It was the very thing.

•••◦◦◗◉◖◦◦•••

The leaf-etched silver bowl was heavy, so Auri made a special trip and carried it two-handed back to Mantle. Next she fetched the large stone mortar where it hunkered down all lurksome in Darkhouse. She went to Clinks and brought two bottles back. She searched the floor of Tenners till she found a scattering of dry pine needles. She brought these back to Mantle too and placed them at the bottom of the cracked clay cup.

By then the fire had faded into ashes. She swept them up. She placed them in the cracked clay cup and packed them tight.

She went to rinse her sooty hands. She rinsed her face and feet.

Auri set another fire and kindled it. She put the suet in the kettle. She hung the kettle by the fire to melt. She added salt. She grinned.

She went down to Tree again and brought back the acorns she had gathered and a wide, flat pan. She shelled the nuts and toasted them, jiggling them about in the pan. She sprinkled them with salt and ate them each by each. Some were bitter. Some were sweet. Some were hardly anything. That was just the way of things.

After she'd eaten them all, she eyed the suet and saw it wasn't finished. Not by half. So one by one she cracked the nutmeg seeds. She ground them in the old stone mortar. She ground them fine as dust and poured the dust into a jar. Crack and grind. Crack and grind. The mortar was a grim thing, thuggish and terse. But after two days without a proper wash, Auri found it perfect suited to her mood.

When she was finished grinding, Auri pulled the

copper pot of melted suet off the fire. She stirred. She sieved the dottle off till there was nothing left but hot, sharp tallow. She set the copper pot aside to cool. She went to fetch fresh water from the proper copper pipe in Pickering. She filled the spirit lamp from a bright steel tap tucked tidily away in Borough.

When she returned, the fire had died again. She swept the ashes up and pressed them down into the cracked clay cup.

She rinsed her sooty hands. She rinsed her face and feet.

She lit the fire a third and final time, then Auri went to Port and eyed her shelves. She brought the bottle of Esther's and set it near the fireplace with her tools. She brought the hollycloth.

Next she carried in the jar of dark blue laurel fruit. But much to her chagrin, it wouldn't fit. No matter how she tried, the jar of laurel simply wouldn't let itself be settled with her tools. Not even when she offered it the mantleplace.

Auri felt unfairly vexed. The laurel would have been ideal. She'd thought of it as soon as she'd awoke and thought of soap. It would have fit like hand into a hand. She'd planned to mingle . . .

But no. There was no place for it. That much was clear. The stubborn thing would simply not be reasoned with.

It exasperated her, but she knew better than to force

the world to bend to her desire. Her name was like an echo of an ache in her. She was unwashed and tangled-haired. It would be nothing but pure folly. She sighed and brought the jar of dark blue fruit back to its shelf in Port where it sat: self-centered and content.

Then Auri sat upon the warm, smooth stones of Mantle. She sat before the fireplace, her makeshift tools laid out around her.

The ashes in the cracked clay cup were just as they should be. Fine and soft. Oak would have made them too intractable. Birch was bitter. But this, this was a perfect mix. Ash and elm and hawthorn. They made a medley without melding or meddling. The ash was proud but not unseemly. The elm was graceful but not inappropriately apetalous, especially for her.

And the hawthorn . . . well. Auri blushed a bit at that. Suffice to say that apetalous or no, she was still a healthy young lady, and there *was* such a thing as too much decorum.

Next she brought out the bottle of Esther's. They were terribly coy, full of stolen moments and the scent of selas flower. Perfect. Thieving was precisely what she needed here.

The nutmeg was foreign, and something of a stranger. It was brimful of sea foam. A lovely addition. Essential. They were cipher *and* a mystery. But that was not particularly troublesome to her. She understood some secrets must be kept.

She peered into the cooling pot and saw the tallow
starting to congeal. It hugged the kettle's edge, making
a slender crescent like the moon. She grinned. Of
course. She had found it underneath the moon. It would
follow the moon, waxing full.

But looking closer, Auri's smile faded. The suet was
clean and strong, but there were no apples in it anymore. Now it was brimming full of age and anger. It
was a thunderstorm of rage.

That wouldn't do at all. She could hardly lave
herself with rage day after day. And with no laurel to
keep it at bay . . . well, she would simply have to
draw the anger out. If not, her soap was worse than
ruined.

Auri went back into Port and looked around. It was
a fairly simple choice. She lifted up the honeycomb and
took a single bite. She closed her eyes and felt herself go
all gooseprickle from the sweetness of it. She could not
help but giggle as she licked it off her lips, almost dizzy
from the work of bees inside her.

After she had sucked all of the sweetness from it,
Auri delicately spat the lump of beeswax out into her
palm. She rolled it in her hands until it made a soft,
round bead.

She gathered up the tallow pot and made her way to
Umbrel. The moon was motherly here, peering kindly
through the grate. The gentle light feathered slantways
down to kiss the stone floor of the Underthing. Auri sat

beside the circle of silver light and gently set the kettle in the center of it.

The cooling tallow now formed a thin white ring around the inside of the copper kettle. Auri nodded to herself. Three circles. Perfect for asking. It was better to be gentle and polite. It was the worst sort of selfishness to force yourself upon the world.

Auri tied the bead of beeswax to a thread and dipped it in the center of the still hot tallow. After several moments, she relaxed to see it working like a charm. She felt the rage congealing, gathering around the wax, heading to it like a bear on hunt for honey.

By the time the circle of moonlight had left the

copper pot behind, every bit of anger had been leached out of the tallow. As neat a factoring as ever hand of man had managed.

Then Auri took the kettle off to Tree and set it in the moving water of the chill-well. Cricket-quick the tallow cooled to form a flat white disk two fingers thick.

Auri carefully lifted the disk of tallow off the surface and poured the golden water underneath away, noting idly that it held a hint of sleep and all the apples too. That was a pity. But it could not be helped, such was the way of things sometimes.

The bead of wax was seething. Now that the anger had been factored free, Auri realized it was much fiercer stuff than she had thought. It was fury, thunderous with untimely death. It was a mother's rage for cubs now left alone.

Auri was glad the bead already dangled from a thread. She would be loath to touch it with her hands.

Slow and quiet, Auri tucked the bead into a thick glass jar and sealed it with a tight, tight lid. This she carried off to Boundary. Oh so careful she carried it. Oh so careful she placed it on a high stone shelf. Behind the glass. It would be safest there.

In Mantle, Auri's third and final fire had fallen into ash. She swept it up again. These ashes filled the cracked clay cup to brimming.

She rinsed her sooty hands. She rinsed her face and feet.

All was ready. Auri grinned and sat down on the warm stone floor with all her tools arrayed around her. On the outside she was all composed, but inside she was fairly dancing at the thought of her new soap.

She set the kettle on the iron tripod. Underneath she slid the spirit lamp so that the hot, bright flame could kiss the copper bottom of the kettle.

First there was her perfect disk of clean white tallow. It was strong and sharp and lovely as the moon. Part of her, some wicked, restless piece, wanted to break the disk to bits so it would melt the faster. So she could have her soap the sooner. So she could wash herself and brush her hair and finally set herself to rights after so long. . . .

But no. She set the tallow gently in the kettle, careful not to give offense. She left it in its pure and perfect circle. Patience and propriety. It was the only graceful thing to do.

Next came the ashes. She set the cracked clay cup atop a squat glass jar. She poured the clear, clean water over them. It filtered through the ash and drip, tick, trickled through the crack in the cup's bottom. It was the smoky red of blood and mud and honey.

When the final drips had fallen, Auri held the jar of cinderwash aloft and saw it was as fine as any she had ever made. It was a sunset dusky red. Stately and graceful, it was a changing thing. But underneath it all, the liquid held a blush of wantonness. It held all the proper things the wood had brought and many caustic lies besides.

In some ways this would be enough. The tallow and the cinderwash would make a serviceable soap. But there would be no apples in it. Nothing sweet or kind. It would be hard and chill as chalk. It would resemble bathing with an indifferent brick.

So yes, in some ways, these would be enough for soap. But how awful would that be? How terrible to live surrounded by the stark, sharp, hollowness of things that simply were *enough*?

Sitting on the warm, smooth floor of Mantle, Auri shivered at the thought of moving through a joyless world like that. Nothing perfect. Nothing beautiful and true. Oh no. She was too wise to live that way. Auri looked around and smiled at all her luxury. She had a perfect loving leaf and lavender. She wore her favorite dress. Her name was Auri, and it was a shining piece of gold inside her all the time.

So she twisted off the silver stopper from the ice-blue jar, and poured the perfume in among the well-ground nutmeg powder. The smell of selas flower filled the room, so sweet and light against the prickle sting of nutmeg.

Auri smiled and stirred the two together with a kindling stick, then poured the thick, wet, pulpy mass into the linen sack she'd set inside a wide-mouthed jar. She used two sticks to twist the ends of the sack, and her makeshift wringer squeezed the fabric tight until it oozed a thick, dark oily liquid that spattered down into the jar. It was barely a slow trickle. Just a spoonful of the liquid. Two spoonfuls. Three.

She turned the sticks, her mouth a line of concentration. The linen twisted tighter. The dark liquid welled up, gathered, dripped. Dripped again.

Despite herself, Auri wished she had a proper press. It was so wasteful otherwise. She strained against the sticks, shifting her grip and giving them another half a turn. She grit her teeth, her knuckles going white. Another drip. Three more. Ten.

Auri's arms began to tremble, and despite herself she glanced toward the iron-bound door that led to Boundary.

She looked away. She was a wicked thing, but she

was not so bad as that. Idle wishing was mere fancy. It was another thing entirely to bend the world toward her own desires.

Finally her shaking arms could bear no more. She sighed, relaxed, and pulled the sticks free, upending the linen sack into a shallow pan. No longer a dark, pulpy mass, the nutmeg pomace now looked pale and crumbly.

Auri lifted up the glass and eyed the viscous liquid, clear as amber. It was lovely, lovely, lovely. It was like nothing that she'd ever seen before. It was thick with secrets and sea foam. It was prickle-rich with mystery. It was full of musk and whispers and tetradecanoic acid.

It was so fine a thing she dearly wished for more of it. The jar hardly held a palmful. She glanced over at the pan and thought of squeezing out the pomace with her hands to gather up a few more precious drops. . . .

But reaching out, Auri found that she was oddly loath to touch the gritty mass with her own naked skin. She paused and tipped her head to look more closely at the pale, grey, crumbling pomace and her stomach pulled into a knot at what she saw.

It was full of screaming. Days of endless dark red screaming. It had been hidden by the mysteries before, but now the selas-sweet had stolen those away, and Auri saw the screaming clear as day.

Auri lifted up the jar and eyed the amber byne. But no. It was just as she had seen before. There was no screaming hidden there among the mysteries and musk. It was still a perfect thing.

Auri drew a long and shaky breath at that. And setting down the jar, she gently lay the linen sack and both her twisting sticks inside the shallow tin pan beside the horrid pomace. She handled them as little as she could, with nothing but her fingertips, as if they had been poisoned.

She did not want it near her. No bit of it. She knew already. She knew of red. She'd had enough of screaming.

Sweating slightly, Auri lifted up the pan with both her hands and turned to face the doorway. Then she stopped before she took a single step toward well-ordered Port. She could not keep this there. Who knew what chaos it would bring? Screaming was no kind of kindly neighbor.

Auri turned toward the hallway then. She took a step, then stopped, not knowing where she'd go. To Billows where the wind would carry screaming all throughout the Underthing? To Tree where it would smolder like a coal, so near her pots and pans and precious peas. . . .

But no. No no.

So Auri turned a final time. She turned to face the third way out of Mantle. She turned toward the iron-bound door and brought the linen bag to Boundary.

••◦◉◦••

Returning, Auri rinsed her face. She rinsed her hands and feet.

She took one step toward the tripod and the copper

pot, then stopped. She went back to her basin. She rinsed her face. She rinsed her hands and feet.

More than anything she wanted soap. To sit and finish what she had begun. She was so close. But first she stepped off hurriedly to Port to make herself quite sure of things. She smoothed the blanket with both hands. She touched the flat grey stone. She moved the hollybottle back where it belonged. She touched the leather book, then opened up the cover to make sure certain its pages were still all uncut. They were. But glancing back toward the shelf she saw the stone had gone all out of joint. She tried to slide it back to proper true but couldn't see the shape of it and couldn't tell the way of things and if it was a place where it was right. The honey too. She wanted honey but she mustn't. . . .

She rubbed her eyes. Then forced herself to stop and look down at her hands. She hurried back to Mantle. She rinsed her face. She rinsed her hands and feet.

She felt the panic rising in her then. She knew. She knew how quickly things could break. You did the things you could. You tended to the world for the world's sake. You hoped you would be safe. But still she knew. It could come crashing down and there was nothing you could do. And yes. She knew she wasn't right. She knew her everything was canted wrong. She knew her head was all unkilter. She knew she wasn't true inside. She knew.

Her breath was coming harder now. Her heart a

hammer in her chest. The light was brighter and she heard the sound of things that normally she couldn't hear. A keening of the world all out of place. A howl of everything all turned from true. . . .

Auri looked around the room, all startle sweat and fear. She was tangle and cut-string. Even here. She could see traces. Mantle was all eggshell. Even her most perfect place. Her bed was almost not her bed. Her perfect leaf so frail. Her box of stone so far away. Her lavender no help at all and growing pale. . . .

She looked down at her shaking hands. Was she all full of screaming now? Again? No. No no. It wasn't her. Not just. It was all everything. All everything unravelding and thin and tatter. She could not even stand. The light was jagged, scraping like a knife against her teeth. And underneath it was the hollow dark. The nameless empty everything was clawing at the fraying edges of the walls. Even Foxen wasn't even nearly. The stones were strange. The air. She went looking for her name and couldn't even find it flickering. She was just hollow in. Everything was. Everything was everything. Everything was everything else. Even here in her most perfect place. She needed. Please she needed please. . . .

But there. Against the wall she saw the brazen gear was all unchanged. It was too full of love. Nothing could shift it. Nothing could turn it from itself. When all the world was palimpsest, it was a perfect palindrome. Inviolate.

It was all the way across the room. So far she feared she could not reach it. Not with the stones below her gone so rough. Not hollow as she was. But when she moved a bit she saw it was not hard at all. It was down-hill. The proud, bright brazen gear was true enough, it pressed down hard against the thin frayed tatter world and made a dent.

Then she was touching it. It was so smooth and warm along its face. And all asweat breathless desper-ate Auri pressed her forehead up against its cool. She took hold of it with both her hands. The sharpness of its edges on her palms was like a calming knife. She clung to it at first, like someone in a shipwreck grips the stone of shore. But all the world around her was still storm. All tumbledown. All crumble pale and ache. And so, with shaking arms she strained against it. She pulled to turn the gear upon its narrow ledge of rock. She spun it widdershins. The breaking way.

It tipped from tooth to tooth. She spun the brazen gear and only then did Auri understand the fearsome weight of it. It was a fulcrum thing. It was a pin. A pivot. It shifted, tilted, but truthfully it only *seemed* to turn. In truth, it stayed. It staid. In truth the whole world spun.

One final weighty tip and now the space left by the missing tooth was turned straight down. And as the edges of the gear grit hard into the stone Auri felt the whole world jar around her. It ticked. Clicked. Fit.

Fixed. Trembling, she looked around and saw that everything was fine. Her bed was just her bed. All of everything in Mantle: fine. Nothing was nothing else. Nothing was anything it shouldn't be.

Auri sat down hard upon the floor. So sudden-full of sweet relief she gasped. She laughed and gathered up the gear and held it to her chest. She kissed it. She closed her eyes and wept.

ALL TO HER DESIRE

SETTING FULCRUM BACK upon his narrow ledge, Auri wiped her smudgy tears away from his sweet brazen face. Then she walked over to the kettle and was pleased to see the tallow was all melted. It smelled of hot, of hearth, of earth, of breath. She bent and puffed the yellow flame away.

Then to her basin. Auri rinsed her face. She rinsed her hands and feet.

She sat herself beside the kettle on the warm stone floor. Soon now. Close. She grinned, and for the space of one long breath she almost didn't mind how tangle-haired and smudged she had become.

Auri stirred the tallow with a slender stick. She drew a calming breath. She took the jar of cinderwash and poured it slowly in among the tallow. The mix went cloudy all at once, white tinged with just a hint of pink. She grinned her proudest grin and stirred and stirred again.

She gathered up the amber byne, all prickling quick and petal kind. She poured it in the kettle too, and all the room was filled with musk and mystery and bear. She stirred and selas filled the air.

Her face intent, once more she stirred. Once more. She felt the mix grow thick. She stopped and set aside the slender stick.

She took a breath and let it out. She went and rinsed her face and hands and feet. Two by two, she gathered up her tools and took them back where they belonged. Back to Tree and Port and Clinks she carried bottles, lamps, and pans.

When all of this was done, Auri took the now-cool copper pot and carried it to Port. She tipped the kettle, reached inside, and lifted out a smooth, curved dome of pale, sweet soap.

She used the flat edge of the petal plate to slice the dome of soap. She cut it into cakes, each one a different size, a different shape. Each to each, and all to her desire. It felt wicked and delicious, but given that the soap was hers, this tiny willfulness could do no harm.

She indulged herself from time to time. It helped remind her she was truly free.

As she worked, Auri saw the soap was not true white. It was the palest pink, the color of fresh cream with just a single drop of blood. Auri lifted up a cake, and moving oh so careful, she brought it to her face and touched it lightly with her tongue.

She grinned at its perfection. It was kissing soap. Soft but firm. Mysterious but sweet. There was nothing like it in all Temerant. Nothing below the earth or underneath the sky.

Auri couldn't wait a moment more. She skipped off to her basin. She washed her face and hands and feet. She laughed. She laughed so sweet and loud and long it sounded like a bell, a harp, a song.

She went to Clinks. She washed herself. She brushed her hair. She laughed and leapt.

She hurried home. She went to bed. And all alone, she smiled and slept.

THE GRACEFUL WAY TO MOVE

THE SIXTH DAY Auri woke, her name unfurling like a flower in her heart.

Foxen felt it too and fairly burst with light when she first wetted him. It was a waxing day. A day for making.

She laughed at that before she even left her bed. The day had come too late, but she could hardly care. Her soap was sweet as any ever was. Besides, there was a dignity to doing things in your own time.

But that thought sobered her somewhat. His visit would not wait. He would be here, soon. Tomorrow. And she still had nothing good enough to share. She had no perfect gift to give.

There were three ways out of Mantle. . . . But no.

She washed her face and hands and feet. She brushed her hair until it was a golden cloud. She took a drink and donned her favorite dress. She didn't dally. Today was going to be a busy day.

First came the disposition of her new and perfect soap. She had made seven cakes. One was by her basin, safe in Mantle. One she'd washed with yesterday in Clinks. The largest four she carried off to Bakery to cure. The smallest, sweetest one she tucked into the bottom of her cedar box so she would never have to go without again. That was a lesson firmly learned. Oh yes.

She paused, one hand inside her cedar box. Would he like a cake of kissing soap? It was quite fine. He never would have seen its like before. . . .

But no. She flushed before she'd even finished thinking it. It would be altogether too improper. Besides, it was not right for him. The mysteries might fit, but he had much of oak about him. Willow too, and he was absolutely *not* a selas sort.

She shut the lid of her sweet cedar box, but getting to her feet, Auri felt the room go bright and tip around her. Staggering, she took two steps and sat down on the bed before she fell. She felt the fear rise up in her. Her eyes darted round the room, all startlement. Was this . . . ?

No. This was a simpler thing, her stomach was an empty drum again. She had forgotten to tend herself.

So when her head stopped spinning, it was off to Tree. But on a whim, for company, she brought along brash Fulcrum. He had seen so little of the Underthing. And heavy as he was, it really was the least that she could do for all his help.

Pans were nearly all the fruit that Tree could offer up.

But only nearly. She brought out a tin pot and filled it with fresh water. She lit the spirit lamp with her penultimate match. Then she climbed onto the counter and reached with both hands to fetch down her jar. The dried peas rolled inside, tinkling playfully against the glass.

She worked the baling top and poured peas into her tiny hand until they filled her cupped palm. Her hand was not that large. It was not so very many peas, but it was half of what she had. She tipped them into the pot where they plinked into the warming water. Then, after a moment's hesitation, Auri shrugged and poured the other half into the pot as well.

She set the empty bottle on the countertop and looked around. The burner's flickerlight and Foxen's green-blue glow both showed the bareness of the shelves. She sighed and put it from her mind. Today there would be soup. Tomorrow he would visit. And after that . . .

Well, after that she would do her best. That was the only way. You did not want things for yourself. That made you small. That kept you safe. That meant you could move smoothly through the world without upsetting every applecart you came across. And if you were careful, if you were a proper part of things, then you could help. You mended what was cracked. You tended to the things you found askew. And you trusted that the world in turn would brush you up against the chance to eat. It was the only graceful way to move. All else was vanity and pride.

Could she bring honeycomb to share with him tomorrow? It was the loveliest of things. He had too little sweetness in his life. That was the truth.

She thought on this while boiling bubbles danced her peas about the pot. Auri idly stroked brash Fulcrum's face, and after a long while of musing she decided, yes, the honeycomb might work if nothing else presented.

She stirred the soup a bit and added salt. She wished the butter wasn't full of knives. A little fat in this would be a true delight. A little fat would suit it to a T.

••••◦◗◦••••

After her lovely soup, Auri headed back to Mantle. With Fulcrum keeping company she could hardly make her way through Vaults or Veneret. So she took the long way round and went by way of Pickering instead.

Belly warm and with a guest besides, she took her time along the close-fit square stone tunnels. She was nearly back to Doubton, Fulcrum heavy in her arms, when she felt a gentle crickling underfoot and stopped.

Looking down, she saw a scattering of leaves upon the floor. It didn't make a bit of sense to find them here. There was no wind in Pickering. No water here. She looked around, but couldn't see a speckle of bird dropping. She sniffed the air but didn't smell a bit of musk or piss.

But there was nothing threatening either. Nothing

knotted up about the place. No skew or wrongness
here. But not nothing neither. It was half a thing. A
mystery.

Curious, Auri set Fulcrum gently down upon the
floor and lifted up the leaf. It looked familiar. She
hunted round and found a handful of them scattered
near an open doorway. She picked these up and when
they wrangled up together in her hand she understood.

Excited, she took Fulcrum back to Mantle. Before
she left she kissed his face and set him comfortably
to rights upon his stony ledge, gap down of course.
Then she skipped to Port and lifted up the silver

bowl. She held the crickling leaf she carried up against the twining leaves engraved around the edge. It was the same.

She shook her head, unsure of what they might portend. Still, there was only one way to tell. Taking up the silver bowl, Auri scurried back to Pickering, then through the doorway where she'd found the clustered leaves. Over a stone tumble. Around a fallen beam.

She did not know if she had ever been to this piece of Pickering before. But it was still simplicity itself to find her way. Here and there, a leaf or two would dot the floor like breadcrumbs.

Finally she came to the bottom of a narrow shaft that led straight up. An ancient chimney from the days before? A tunnel for escape? A well?

It was narrow and steep, but Auri was a tiny thing. And even carrying the silver bowl she climbed it quickly as a squirrel. At the top she found a plank of wood, already partially askew. She pushed it easily aside and clambered out into a basement room.

The room was dusty and disused, full of shelves. Barrels stacked in corners. Shelves jammed full with bundles, kegs, and crates. In among the smell of dust she caught a whiff of street and sweat and grass. Looking round she saw a window high up in the wall, and on the floor below some broken glass.

It was a tidy place, save for a scattering of leaves blown down in some forgotten storm. There were sacks of corn and barley flour. Winter apples. Waxed packages stuffed tight with figs and dates.

Auri walked around the room, her hands behind her back. She stepped lightly as a dancer on a drum. Kegs of molasses. Jars of strawberry preserve. Some squash had tumbled from their burlap bundle just beside the door. She shooed them back inside and pulled the drawstring tight.

Eventually she bent to look more closely at a lower shelf. A single leaf had come to rest atop a small clay crock. Moving carefully, she lifted up the leaf, removed the crock, and put the silver bowl down in its place. She lay the leaf back down inside the bowl.

She allowed herself a single longing look around the room, no more. Then Auri headed back the way she came. Only back in the familiar dark of Pickering did she draw an easy breath. Then eagerly she brushed the dust from her new treasure. If the picture was to be believed, the crock held olives. They were lovely.

••••••••••

The olives went to Tree. They looked a little lonely on their shelf. But lonely was a long sight better than naught but empty echo, salt, and butter full of knives. Better by a long road.

Next she checked on things in Port. The ice-blue bottle wasn't entirely at home. It huddled on the lowest, leftest shelf upon the eastern wall. Auri touched it gently, doing her best to reassure. He liked bottles. Might this be a seemly gift?

She picked it up and turned it in her hands. But no. Not this bottle. Grave. Graven. Not named for someone else.

Maybe some other bottle? That felt nearly right. Not quite, but nearly.

She thought about the vanity in Tumbrel. Yesterday it had seemed squared and true. But she was more than slightly tattered then. Not at her best. Perhaps there was a bottle mixed among the rest. Something wrong or lost or out of place.

If nothing else it was a place to start. So Auri gathered up the warm, sweet weight of Fulcrum in her arms. And because he hadn't seen them yet, she took the slightly longer way through Van and Forth and Lucient before she headed down to Wains.

She paused to rest in Annulet, her new and perfect circle of a sitting room. Fulcrum settled like a king upon the velvet chair while Auri lounged upon the fainting couch and let her arms recover from the oh sweet ache of holding him.

But she was too busy for long lounging. So Auri gathered up the heavy gear again and made her slow way up the unnamed stair, taking her time so Fulcrum could marvel at the odd and cunning coyness of the place. And, as the two of them were gentle folk, they both ignored the bashful door that sat upon the landing.

Then into Tumbrel. Climbing through the wall, Auri saw the room was just as she remembered. Not perfect true like Annulet. But nothing glaringly unskew. Nothing askant or lost or loudly wrong. Now that the vanity was squared away, Tumbrel seemed content to rumble down into a long warm winter's sleep.

Even so, she'd come all this way. So she opened up the wardrobe and peered inside. She touched the chamberpot. She looked into the closet too, nodding politely to the broom and bucket there.

Auri eyed the vanity. There were a few fine bottles there. One especially caught her eye. It was small and pale. Coruscant, like opal. Perfect with a cunning clasp. She didn't have to open it to see that there was breath inside. A precious thing.

She lifted Fulcrum higher and tried peering through the round hole in the very center of his oh so centeredness. She hoped to notice something she had missed before. Something loose or raveledy. Some thread that she could tug to jostle something free. But no. Whether she looked straight or slant, the vanity was well and truly set to rights.

A bottle coruscant with hidden breath would be a princely gift. But no. Taking it was every bit as stupid and unkind as wrenching out a tooth so she could carve a bead from it and thread it on a string.

She sighed and left. Out through the wall, then down the unnamed stair. Perhaps she could go hunting down in Lynne, it was a piping place, and mus—

It was then. Heading down, a sly stone turned beneath her foot. As Auri made her musing way from Tumbrel down the unnamed stair, a stone step tipped and pitched. Her forward. Lurching.

Auri gave a cry, and in her sudden startle Fulcrum leapt away. He spun and tumbled from her arms and sailed out from the cloud of her gold hair. Heavy as he was, he almost seemed to float rather than fall. He turned, toppled, and struck the seventh stair so hard he cracked the stone and bounded back into the air, then spun again, fell flat upon his brazen face, and shattered on the landing.

The sound he made was like the keening of a broken bell. The sound was like a dying harp. Bright pieces scattered when he struck the stone.

Auri somehow kept her feet. She didn't fall, but oh, her heart went icy in her chest. She sat down hard upon the steps. Too numb to walk. Her heart was cold and white as chalk.

She could still feel him in her hands. She saw the lines of his sharp edges kissed into her skin. Coming to her feet she shuffled stiffly down the stairs. Her steps were numb and stumbling as more thoughtless step-stones tried to trip her, like a daft old man who won't stop telling an unfunny joke yet and again.

She knew. She should have moved more gently with the world. She knew the way of things. She knew if you weren't always stepping lightly as a bird the whole world came apart to crush you. Like a house of cards. Like a bottle against stones. Like a wrist pinned hard beneath a hand with the hot breath smell of want and wine. . . .

All brittle stiff, Auri came to stand upon the bottom stair. Her eyes were down and all around her hung her sunny hair. This was the worst of wrong. She could not bring herself to look beyond her tiny dust-smudged feet.

But there was nothing else to do. She lifted up her eyes and peered. Then peeked. Then she saw the pieces, and her heart went sideways in her chest. No. Not shattered. Broken. He had broken.

Slowly Auri's face broke too. It broke into a grin so wide you'd think she ate the moon. Oh yes. Fulcrum had broken, but that wasn't *wrong*. Eggs break. Horses break. Waves break. Of course he broke. How else could someone so all certain-centered let his perfect answers out into the world? Some things were just too true to stay.

Fulcrum lay in three bright pieces. Three jagged shapes with three teeth each. No longer a pin stuck hard into the heart of things. He had become three threes.

If anything her grin grew wider then. Oh. Oh. Oh. Of course. It wasn't some*thing* she was looking for. No wonder all her searching was for naught. No wonder everything was canted wrong. It was *three* things. He was bringing *three*, and so must she. Three perfect threes would be her gift for him.

Auri's brow furrowed and she turned to look back up the stairs. The gear had struck the seventh step. Fulcrum had shattered it quite flagrantly. Not seven then. Another thing she had been wrong about. He wasn't coming on the seventh day. He would visit her *today*.

Some other time that knowing might have sent her spinning badly out of true. It would have set her all asweat and tangled beyond all hope. But not today. Not with the truth so sweetly set before her. Not with everything so sudden plain for her to see. Three things was *easy* if you knew the way of it.

Auri was so whelmed it took her several minutes before she realized where she was standing. Or rather, she realized that the stairway finally knew where it was. Knew *what* it was. Where it belonged. It had a name. She was in Ninewise.

THE HIDDEN HEART OF THINGS

AURI GATHERED UP the threes and headed back to Mantle. They seemed much lighter now, though that was no surprise. They had spilled their secrets, and Auri knew full well how heavy hard-held secrets could become.

Back in Mantle, Auri carefully arrayed the threes. But before she even finished settling them along the wall, she saw the shape of her first gift to him. It couldn't be more clear. No wonder there was so much extra floor in here. No wonder she had never used the second shelf along the wall.

The teeth were marvelous. So true. They shone like wishes from a faerie tale.

Seeing how it ought to be, Auri took the first bright three straight back to Tumbrel. Through Wains with its altogether men, and circle-perfect Annulet, then Nine-wise, all nonchalant with its new-namedness.

Grinning, Auri carried the bright brass three right up to the wardrobe drawer and tucked it in most carefully. It nestled in effortlessly. It fit there like a lover or a key. She reached down with both hands and felt the cool white smoothness of the sheet against her fingertips. She brought it up and pressed it to her lips.

It was free to leave. And breathless, she came running back to Mantle with it clutched against her chest.

The second three she carried straightaway to Tocks. And for a breathless moment Auri left the Underthing behind. A broken wall, a hidden stair, then through a basement up into the store room of the finest inn she knew. There she left the three and took away a thick white eider stuffed with innocence and down. It was fine and soft, full of kind whispers and remembered roads.

Even laden with the weight of it, Auri sprinted through the tunnels lightly as a wisp.

Back in Mantle, she spread the mattress carefully against the wall across from her own bed. Close enough that if he needed her just whispering would be enough. Close enough so if he wanted to, he could sing to her at night.

She flushed a bit on thinking that, then brought the perfect creamy sheet and wrapped it all around his bed. She smoothed it gently with her hands. Its loveliness was like a kiss against her skin.

Grinning, Auri crossed to Port and brought the

blanket back. No wonder it had left her. It had known the truth of things much sooner than herself. It simply wasn't for her anymore. She spread his blanket on the bed and noticed it no longer feared the floor. Stepping back she looked at it, so soft and sweet and safe and fair.

From Port she brought his fine teacup. She brought the leather book, uncut, unread, and utterly unknown. She brought the small stone figurine. All three of these she set upon the shelf beside his bed so he would have some beauty of his own.

And just like that, she had a gift for him: a safe place he could stay.

As much as she might want to stop and bask, she needed to keep moving. Three was the rule today. She needed two gifts more.

⸺•◦●◦•⸺

Auri went back to Port and eyed the shelves with her best maker's eye. And since it was a making day, and with the wind so fair upon her back, she thought on what it was that he might need.

It was a different way of thinking. Even though she was not wanting for herself, she knew this sort of thing was dangerous.

She eyed the hollybottle, it teased at her, but she knew it wasn't right for him. Not quite. It was an unexpected visit gift. The honeycomb . . . almost. She reached out to touch two fingers to the jar of laurel fruit. She lifted up the jar and held it to the light. It's true that he was somewhat lacking laurels.

It clicked together then. Of course. She smiled a bit. What better to keep rage at bay? Besides, it was the third part of a thing she'd already begun. A candle. A candle would be just the thing for him.

She stopped then, all of a sudden, the jar still in her hand. She held her breath and thought about the hard realities of time. A candle meant melting. And melding. Most of all it meant a mold. She felt her whole face frowning at the thought of something dipped for him. It wasn't right at all, he was not one for dribs and drabs.

No. A mold. It was the only way to make a candle fine enough for him.

And that meant Boundary.

She didn't hardly hesitate at all. For herself she would not dare, but this was simply how it had to be. Didn't he deserve a few fine things? After all that he had done, didn't he deserve a fine and princely gift?

Of course he did. So Auri strode to Mantle. So Auri opened wide the iron-bound door. So Auri entered Boundary.

•••◆◗◐◗◆•••

It was a clean and quiet place.

There was a workbench. It was dark and smooth and hard as stone. There were mountings on the sides. A vice. A set of floating rings. A burner stand. There were taps and faucets, well-arrayed: all steel and brass and iron.

There were shelves here, all mounted on one wall. Crowded with vast and varied tools of the craft. Acids and re-agents in their stoppered glasses. Sulfonium inside a jar of stone. Racks of pow-ders, salts and earths and herbs. Oils and unguents.

Fourteen waters. Twicelime. Camphor. All perfect. All true. All gathered and factored and stored in the most proper ways.

There were tools here. Alembics and retorts. A fine wide wickless burner. Coils of copper tubing. Crucibles and tongs and boiling baths. There were sieves and filters and copper knives. There was a fine grinder and a gleaming clean screw press.

There were the stone shelves too. The careful shelves. Bottles hunkered there behind the thick, thick glass. These bottles were not tidy like the other shelves. They were not labeled. They were muttly. One held screaming. Another, fury. There were many bottles there, and those two were nowhere near the worst.

Auri set the jar of laurel fruit atop the workbench. She was a small thing. Urchin small. Most things did not fit her. Most tables were too tall. This one was not.

This room used to belong to her. But no. This room belonged to someone once. Now it didn't. It wasn't. It was a none place. It was an empty sheet of nothing that could not belong. It was not for her.

Auri opened a drawer in the workbench and brought out a circtangular brass mold. The sort that would suit a candle well.

Her expression grave, Auri eyed the laurel fruit. It was every bit as reverent as one might expect, but it was prideful too. And held a hint of north wind's chill. That needed to be tempered. And . . . yes. There was a thread of anger running through it too. She sighed. That would not do at all.

She narrowed her eyes at it and danced the numbers through her head. Glancing back and forth between the mold and the jar of fruit, she saw the wax it bore would not be near enough. Not for an entire candle. Not for a proper candle. Not for him.

Auri left and returned with the honeycomb. Moving in a businesslike fashion, she lay it in the press and screwed the handle down until the honey poured into the clear, clean jar below. It was the work of half a minute.

Leaving it to drip, she lit the nearby wickless and spun the ringstand so that it held a crucible at the proper height. She opened up the press, lifted out the flat sheet of beeswax, and folded it in quarters before setting it in the crucible. There was not a lot of it, perhaps as much as she could cup in both her hands. But once she'd rendered down the laurel fruit, it would be enough to fill the mold.

Auri eyed the melting wax and nodded. It was a drowsy thing. All autumn sweetness, diligence, and due reward. The bells were not unwelcome either. There was nothing in it that she did not want for him.

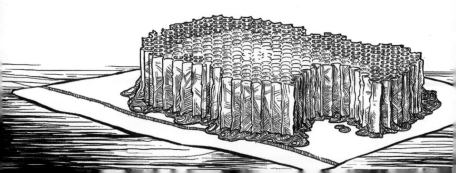

Honey and laurel might have been enough if this were a simple poet's candle. But he was no mere poet. She needed something more.

A pinch of camphor would have been ideal. Just a pinch, a spark, a hint of something volatile. But she had no camphor, and there was no sense in wishing. So she fetched a daub of perfect pitch instead from Port. For binding, and to keep his heart hearty against the coming winter.

Auri stirred the beeswax with a slender glass rod. She smiled. It was a rare joy working with the proper tools. What luxury. Waiting for the resin to dissolve, Auri whistled as she stirred, and grinned. That would be her secret. There would be her whistle in the candle too.

She stepped into Mantle then, and eyed her perfect lavender in the grey glass jar. She lifted out a sprig of it. Then two. Then Auri felt the hot shame rise in her chest. This was no time for thrift. *He* was never stingy with his help. Didn't he deserve sweet dreams?

Auri set her jaw and pulled fully half the lavender from out the jar. She could be a greedy, greedy thing at times.

Back into Boundary. Auri poured the laurel fruit into the grinder. In three breaths' time it was minced tidily and fine. Then she stopped, staring at the mass of half-pulped fruit.

She knew the proper way for laurel. She knew the

patient way of things. Grind and boil the waxy fruit. Sieve off the dottle. Boil again and clarify and cool to separate the wax. Even with the proper tools it would be hours of work. Hours and hours.

But he was coming *soon*. She knew. She knew she had no time for it.

And even if she had all day. There would be principles inside the wax that were not right for him. He was plum full of anger and despair. And pride . . . well, he had that in a sure and certain surfeit.

There were ways to factor those things out. She knew them all. She knew the turning circles of the calcinate. She could sublime and draw. She could isolate a non-exclusionary principle as well as any who had ever turned their hand to work the craft.

But this was not a time for begging favors from the moon. Not now. She could not rush and neither could she be delayed. Some things were simply too important.

It was just as Mandrag said: nine tenths of alchemy was chemistry. And nine tenths of chemistry was waiting.

The other piece? That slender tenth that set it all apart? The heart of alchemy was something Auri had

learned long ago. She'd studied it before she came to understand the true shape of the world. Before she knew the key to being small.

Oh yes. She'd learned her craft. She knew its hidden roads and secrets. All the subtle, sweet, and coaxing ways that made one skilled within the art. So many different ways. Some folk inscribed, described. There were symbols. Signifiers. Byne and binding. Formulae. Machineries of maths . . .

But now she knew much more than that. So much of what she'd thought was truth before was merely tricks. No more than clever ways of speaking to the world. They were a bargaining. A plea. A call. A cry.

But underneath, there was a secret deep within the hidden heart of things. Mandrag never told her that. She did not think he knew. Auri found that secret for herself.

She knew the true shape of the world. All else was shadow and the sound of distant drums.

Auri nodded to herself. Her tiny face was grave. She scooped the waxy fine-ground fruit into a sieve and set the sieve atop a gather jar.

She closed her eyes. She drew her shoulders back. She took a slow and steady breath.

There was a tension in the air. A weight. A wait. There was no wind. She did not speak. The world grew stretched and tight.

Auri drew a breath and opened up her eyes.

Auri was urchin small. Her tiny feet upon the stone were bare.

Auri stood, and in the circle of her golden hair she grinned and brought the weight of her desire down full upon the world.

And all things shook. And all things knew her will. And all things bent to please her.

•••◦●◦•••

It was not long before Auri returned to Mantle with a sorrel-colored candle pressed with lavender. It smelled of bay and bees. It was a perfect thing.

Auri washed her face. She washed her hands and feet.

Soon. She knew. Soon he would come visiting. Incarnadine and sweet and sad and broken. Just like her. He would come, and like the proper gentleman he was, he would bring three things.

Grinning, Auri fairly danced. She would have three things for him as well.

First his clever candle, all Taborlin. All warm and stuffed with poetry and dreams.

Second was a proper place. A shelf where he could put his heart. A bed to sleep. Nothing could harm him here.

And the third thing? Well . . . She ducked her face and felt a slow flush climb her cheeks. . . .

Stalling, Auri reached out for the small stone soldier sitting on his bedshelf. Strange she'd never noticed the design upon its shield. It was so faint. But yes. There was the tower wrapped up in a tongue of flame. No mere soldier, it was a small stone Amyr.

Peering closer, Auri spied slight lines upon his arms as well. She did not know how she had missed these things before. It was a tiny Ciridae. Of course. Of course it was. It would hardly be a proper present for him otherwise. She kissed the tiny figurine and set it back upon the shelf.

Still, there was the third thing. This time Auri did not blush. She smiled. She washed her face and hands and feet. Then she skipped quickly into Port and opened up the hollybottle. With two fingers Auri lifted out a single seed. The tiny berry bright as blood despite green Foxen's light.

Auri scampered off to Van and peered into the mirror. She licked her lips and pressed the berry up against them, daubing it from left to right. Then she smoothed the berry back and forth across them.

She eyed her reflection. She looked no different than before. Her lips were palest pink. She smiled.

Auri returned to Mantle. She washed her face and hands and feet.

Excitement bubbling up inside of her, Auri looked at his bed. His blanket. His bedshelf with the tiny Amyr waiting there to guard him.

It was perfect. It was right. It was a start. He would need a place someday, and it was here all ready for him. Someday he would come, and she would tend to him. Someday he would be the one all eggshell hollow empty in the dark.

And then . . . Auri smiled. Not for herself. No. Not ever for herself. She must stay small and tucked away, well-hidden from the world.

But for him it was a different thing entire. For him she would bring forth all her desire. She would call up all her cunning and her craft. Then she would make a name for him.

Auri spun about three times. She smelled the air. She grinned. All around her everything was proper true. She knew exactly where she was. She was exactly where she ought to be.

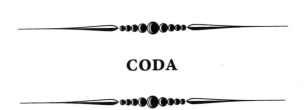

CODA

DEEP IN THE UNDERTHING, stones warm beneath her feet, Auri heard a faint, sweet strain of music.

AUTHOR'S ENDNOTE:

LET ME TELL you a story about a story. Because that's what I do.

••••◊•••

Back in January of 2013, I was in a San Francisco bar with Vi Hart: mathemusician, videotrix, and all-around lovely person. We'd both been fans of each other's work for years without knowing it, and had recently been introduced by a mutual friend.

This was our first time meeting in person. I had just finished the first draft of the story you now hold, and Vi had agreed to take a look at it and give me her opinion.

We spent a couple hours talking about the story, our conversation frequently tangenting off in odd directions, the way good conversations do.

Her feedback was really good. Not just clever, but startlingly insightful. When I mentioned this to her, she looked slightly amused and explained that writing was most of what she did. She scripted her videos, then recorded them. The scripting was the lion's share of the work.

She pointed out some things that needed work in the story, some rough spots, some logical incongruities. She pointed out the parts she liked, too, and talked about the story as a whole.

I should mention that by this point in the evening, I was slightly drunk. A bit of a rarity for me. But since we were hanging out in a bar, it seemed polite to buy a drink. Then I had a drink because Vi was having another, and I wanted to be social. Then I had another because I was a little nervous about meeting Vi for the first time. Then I had another because I was a little nervous about my story.

Well, let's be honest, I was more than a little nervous about the story. I knew, deep in my heart of hearts, that my new-wrought story was a train wreck. A colossal, smoldering mess of a train wreck.

"It doesn't do the things a story is supposed to do," I said to her. "A story should have dialogue, action, conflict. A story should have *more than one character*. I've written a thirty-thousand-word vignette!"

Vi said she liked it.

"Well, yes," I said. "I like it too. But that doesn't matter. You see, people expect certain things from a story," I explained. "You can leave out one or two if you step carefully, but you can't ditch *all* of them. The closest thing I have to an action scene is someone making soap. I spend eight pages describing someone making soap. Eight pages of a sixty-page story making soap. That's something a crazy person does."

As I've said, I was really worried about the story. And perhaps more than slightly drunk. And I was finally getting something off my chest that I hadn't really shared with anyone before.

"People are going to read this and be pissed," I said.

Vi looked at me with serious eyes. "I felt more of an emotional connection to the inanimate objects in this story than I usually feel toward entire characters in other books," she explained. "It's a good story."

But I wasn't having any of it. I shook my head, not even looking up at her. "Readers expect certain things. People are going to read this and be disappointed. It doesn't do what a normal story is supposed to do."

Then Vi said something I will always remember. "Fuck those people," she said. "Those people have stories written for them all the time. What about me? Where's the story for people like me?"

Her voice was passionate and hard and slightly angry. She might have slammed her hand down on the table at this point. I like to think she slammed her hand down on the table. Let's say she did.

"Let those other people have their normal stories," Vi said. "This story isn't *for* them. This is my story. This story is for people like me."

It was one of the nicest things anyone has ever said to me.

•••◗◗●◗••

I did not mean to write this story. Or rather, I did not mean to have this story about Auri turn out the way it did.

I started writing it midway through 2012. I meant for it to be a short story for the *Rogues* anthology edited by George Martin and Gardner Dozois. I'd anticipated it being a trickster story and figured Auri would make a nice complement to the more traditional scoundrel-type rogues who would no doubt show up in that book.

But the story didn't turn out the way I'd expected. It was stranger than a simple trickster tale, and Auri herself was more full of secrets and mysteries than I had guessed.

Eventually the Auri story hit 14,000 words, and I abandoned it. It was too long. Too odd. And beside all that, it had become clear it wasn't right for the anthology. Auri was no mere trickster. Most importantly, this wasn't a rogue story at all.

Despite the fact that I was already over deadline, Martin and Gardner were very kind and gave me some extra time. So I wrote "The Lightning Tree" instead, a story featuring Bast. A much better fit for the anthology.

But Auri's story was still crawling around in my head, and I realized the only way to get it out was to finish the thing. Besides, I owed Bill Schafer at Subterranean Press a novella from *way* back. He'd published my two not-for-children picture books, *The Adventures of the Princess and Mr. Whiffle: The Thing Beneath the Bed*, and the sequel, *The Dark of Deep Below*. So I knew he wasn't afraid of a story that was a little strange.

So I kept writing the story, and it kept getting longer, and stranger. I could tell by this point that it wasn't any sort of normal. It wasn't doing the things a proper sort of story should do. It was, by all traditional metrics, a mess.

But here's the thing. I liked it. It was weird and wrong and tangled and missing so many things that a story is supposed to need. But it kinda worked. Not only was I learning a lot about Auri and the Underthing, but the story itself had a sort of sweetness to it.

Whatever reason, I let the story develop according to its own desire. I didn't force it into a different shape or put anything into it just because it was supposed to be there. I decided to let it be itself. At least for now. At least until I made it to the end. Then I knew I'd probably have to wield the editorial hatchet, performing cruel surgery in order to turn it into something normal. But not yet.

You see, I'd actually been down this road before.

The Name of the Wind does a lot of things it's not supposed to. The prologue is a laundry list of things you should never do as a writer. But despite all that, it works. Sometimes a story works *because* it's different. Maybe this was that kind of story. . . .

But when I wrote the eight-page scene with Auri making soap I realized that was not the case. I was writing a trunk story. For those of you who don't know the term, a trunk story is something you write, then when it's finished you put the manuscript in the bottom of a trunk and forget about it. It's not the sort of story you can sell to a publisher. Not the sort of story people want to read. It's the sort of story that you write, then on your deathbed you remember it and ask a close friend to burn all your unpublished papers. Right after they clear your browser history, of course.

I knew Bill at Sub Press was delightfully open to strange projects, but this? No. No, this was a story I had to write to get out of my head. I had to write it to learn about Auri and the world. (Which is named Temerant, by the way, did you catch that?)

Simply said, I knew this story was for me. It wasn't for other people. Sometimes that happens.

But still, I liked it. It was strange and sweet. I'd finally found Auri's voice. I'm rather fond of her. And I'd learned a lot about writing in the third person, so it wasn't a total waste of time.

When it was finished, I sent it to my agent, Matt,

because that's what you're supposed to do when you're a writer. I told him I was going to offer it to Bill, but that I didn't expect Bill would actually want it, as it was, narratively speaking, a train-wreck.

But Matt read it and liked it.

He gave me a call and said we should send it to Betsy, my editor at DAW.

"She isn't going to want this," I said. "It's a mess. It's the story a crazy person writes."

Matt reminded me that, according to my contracts, Betsy had right of first refusal on any future books I wrote. "Besides," he said. "It's just polite to loop her in. She's your primary publisher."

I shrugged and told him to go ahead and send it. Slightly embarrassed to think of Betsy reading it.

But then Betsy read it and liked it. She really liked it. She wanted to publish it.

That's when I started to sweat.

•••◗◗◗◉◖◖•••

In the many months since my conversation with Vi Hart, I've revised this story roughly eighty times. (This isn't unusual for me. In fact, it's a little on the light side.)

As part of this process, I've given this story to about three dozen beta readers, gathering feedback to help me in my endless, obsessive revisions. And one comment people have made over and over again and again, phrased many different ways, is this:

"I don't know what other people will think. They probably won't like it. But I really enjoyed it."

It's strange to me how many people have said some version of that. Hell, I just now realize I said something similar myself a page or two ago in this author's note.

The truth is, I'm fond of Auri. I have a special place in my heart for this strange, sweet, shattered girl. I love her more than just a little.

I think it's because we're both somewhat broken, in our own odd ways. More importantly, we're both aware of it. Auri knows she isn't all quite proper true inside, and this makes her feel very much alone.

I know how she feels.

But that itself is not unusual. I am the author, after all. I'm *supposed* to know how the character feels. It wasn't until I started gathering feedback that I realized how common this feeling is. I've had person after person tell me that they empathize with Auri. That they know where she's coming from.

I didn't expect that. I cannot help but wonder how many of us walk through our lives, day after day, feeling slightly broken and alone, surrounded all the time by others who feel exactly the same way.

So. If you read this book and you didn't enjoy it, I'm sorry. It's my fault. This is a strange story. You *might* enjoy it more on a second reading. (Most of my stories are better the second time around.) But then again, maybe not.

If you're one of the people who found this story dis-concerting, off-putting, or confusing, I apologize. The truth is, it probably just wasn't for you. The good news is that there are many other stories out there that are written just for you. Stories you will enjoy much more.

This story is for all the slightly broken people out there.

I am one of you. You are not alone. You are all beautiful to me.

Pat Rothfuss

June, 2014

P. S. I realize now that I haven't talked about the illus-trations at all, which is a terrible shame. Not only be-cause they are lovely. And not only because Nathan Taylor is a saint for putting up with my obsessive insanity. But because the story of how they came to be included in this story is an interesting one in its own right . . . .

Unfortunately, I'm out of time and out of space. So that story will have to wait until I write about it on my blog. If you're interested, you can track it down there: http://www.patrickrothfuss.com.